Ballads
and
Bloodshed

Dan DeKoning

Cover Design by GetCovers

ISBN: 978-1-963691-07-8

DEDICATION

This book is dedicated to everyone who enjoys reading a good mystery.

And to all the writers who create them.

Ballads
and
Bloodshed

CHAPTER ONE

I caught my reflection in the side mirror of the bus as we rolled down the highway, and my small, elfin face looked back at me. The window was partially open, so the passing wind threw my hair in various directions, making me look like a modern-day Medusa. I undid the hair band I hadn't taken the time to put on correctly in the first place, closed the window, corralled my unruly locks, and slipped the band over my head.

I looked over at the driver, who appeared, to my delight, to be keeping his eyes on the road. "Do you think I need a color change?"

Bozeman James glanced over long enough to make it appear he was looking at me. He shrugged his shoulders, which signified his typical response since he didn't talk much. Occasionally, when he had too much to drink, he would ramble on for an hour or more, but those moments were few and far between.

"What do you think?" he asked, returning his attention to the highway.

Another Bozeman trait, passing the question right back to

me, and he should have, since I was going to do what I wanted to do, anyway. I checked my locks in the mirror again and paid close attention to where my hair reached the scalp. The first little bits of gray and white peeked through. I could go another week or two, and afterwards I'd have to change, but until that time, I remained happy with the current color, which was a light, almost ice blue. Thanks to poor genetics, I started going gray in my mid-twenties. Since no one wants to see a young country singer with gray hair, I keep it dyed, and usually I go for different colors when I do so, simply to mix it up. Other than the dyed hair, I'm your sweet, run-of-the-mill traveling musician and cowgirl poet.

"I think I'll give it a couple weeks and I'll switch it out to something else. Perhaps a shade of green next time or pink. Perhaps orange."

Bozeman grunted. "You hated orange the last time you tried it."

"Did I?" I wasn't being coy. I honestly didn't remember. I'd have to check the book. Each time I did my hair, I made a brief note in a notebook to describe the specific color and whether I liked the result. Ah, well, that remained a debate for another day.

"Have we ever been to Sunny Station before?" I couldn't remember. Since Bozeman drove the bus, he had a better idea of where we'd been in the past, since he had to pay attention to the road. I, the owner of the shotgun seat, spent my time napping, reading, or looking out the window as we traveled the country's highways and byways from gig to gig.

"No, we haven't," he said.

Sunny Station was a small town nestled south of the San Bernardino National Forest, east of Los Angeles, west of Palm Springs.

"Why is your friend having the release party there instead of L.A.?" I asked.

"He's from there. He titled his new album *Going Home Again,* or something like that, so he thought it would be a good gimmick to have the first release party there. I think the studio's giving him another one in the city in a few days, but he put this one together for his family and friends to get a preview of the album."

"Nice of him to invite us to play," I said.

Bozeman nodded. "Yeah, it's gracious of him. We're only the opening act though, so we'll only get to play for a half hour or forty-five minutes."

I smiled. "That's long enough." I knew it took little effort to get new fans if you had a great sound and presented yourself in an open and fun manner. Even a couple of songs generated enough interest for some people to buy CDs or other merchandise or sign up for our social media sites. It always made me happy to expand our fan base, and even as something as simple as being an opening act would accomplish that.

I knew we weren't getting paid a fortune for this gig. In fact, we'd barely make enough to break even considering the cost of gas and how much it took to feed the bus, but that was okay, because I loved to play.

I got that love of music from my mom, who worked as a traveling musician herself until she met my dad and settled down in Denver with him. She taught me how to play piano, and later, guitar. Mom taught me all about music theory and all the technical stuff that goes into it that no casual listener ever thinks about. She taught me about songwriting, and how a country song, especially, was really about telling a story that condensed down to three minutes. It was tough work, but I loved it, even as a kid, and when I was little, I used to dream about being a country star someday.

I remembered my first songs I played for a room full of other kids in my middle school talent show. I dressed up like Dale Evans, in a white cowgirl outfit. Complete with the strips of leather fringe dangling from the arms and legs, white boots, and a white cowgirl hat to match. Mom bejeweled the outfit with rhinestones, of course. We even decked out my guitar, with my name, Codi Lynn Cassidy, written on the body. I had a little stage fright at first, but when I saw my mom and dad out there in the audience, I got even more nervous.

Then I played my first chord.

My mom had told me that once you strum the guitar, the muscle memory takes over and the nerves go away. But of course, I didn't believe her. She was right, though, and all my stress melted away with the first chord I struck. My set comprised two Dolly Parton numbers, and I won third place. You would think they'd just inducted me into the Country Music Hall of Fame with the praise I got from both my parents.

As time passed, I adopted more of a traditional cowgirl look. I dropped the rhinestones and sequins for blue jeans and non-frilly shirts. The cowgirl boots and hat stayed a part of my stage persona, but when I'm not performing, I like to go with a pair of comfortable sneakers and a baseball cap. Oh, and I dropped the 'Lynn' from my stage name, and now I only go by Codi Cassidy because I'm a sucker for alliteration.

"You know if he wants covers, or can we do original material?" I asked.

Although Bozeman offered some input, I usually came up with the set list, and I normally liked to have it figured out at least a day or two before the show.

"Usual set is fine," he said.

The usual set meant we would go on the heavy side with our original materials, with a couple of covers thrown in. Typically, I did a Willie Nelson tune, but we stayed versatile enough to do about anything, including a couple of pop-rock numbers if we needed to. When I added the covers to the plan, I usually put two or three numbers in the slot, so we decided on stage what to sing. It all depended on the audience, really. If it skewed older, I'd break out some Reba McEntire, or Tanya Tucker. If it tended to be a younger crowd, Carrie Underwood or

Taylor Swift. Sometimes, if Bozeman was in the mood, he'd pick a number for himself and would sing anything from Elvis to Garth Brooks. In the end, it was all about having fun, and if Bozeman and I had a good time, that usually caught on like wildfire with the audience, and they would have a great time, too. The usual set worked great for me, since it took little work for me to pull it together.

"When are we going to be there?" I asked.

Bozeman grunted his usual response when I asked that question. Okay, I asked it more to annoy him than anything. From where I sat, I could easily see the GPS, and according to that, we were almost where we needed to be, which was a county park about a mile or so outside of town.

"Are you going be able to play tomorrow night?" he asked as he checked all the side mirrors for cars in his blind spot.

In response, I rotated my shoulder and stretched out both my arms. I still had a sore arm where I had taken a bullet less than a week before, but I wasn't stiff anymore, and I felt good. "Sure thing. Don't you worry about me."

Bozeman grunted again. That one translated into 'he didn't believe me'.

"After we're parked, I'll play a few songs for you. If you're not satisfied with my performance, we can call in a session guitarist, okay? Deal?"

Bozeman nodded. "Deal. Hold on."

We had arrived at the park, so Bozeman turned the wheel and the bus followed. The park had a gravel road with a myriad of potholes that Bozeman navigated around like a downhill slalom skier at the Olympics. The front wheel on my side dipped into and out of a hole, and I bounced in my seat. I caught the sly smile on Bozeman's face once I settled back into my spot.

Bozeman followed the road past a baseball diamond to the parking area. There were two sizeable areas marked off, and each had a sign next to it. Bozeman did a wide arc, so we'd be facing out and parked the bus next to the sign that had his name stenciled on it. He turned off the ignition and exhaled. The ride from New Mexico had taken only ten hours, including a couple of stops along the way, but I could tell Bozeman seemed tired. He often reminded me that being behind the wheel of a thirty-foot tour bus wasn't quite the same as driving the family sedan. I had to take his word for it, since he didn't allow me to drive the bus. At four-foot-ten and with a skinny physique, I couldn't easily handle the beast. Although I was good for a quick jaunt, I certainly couldn't handle it across the interstates of America. Besides, I never judged the turns around corners quite right, and often drove over curbs, which, for some odd reason, made Bozeman really nervous.

It was mid-afternoon, and a warm, blue-skied day when I stepped off the bus. I walked in circles for a bit, then did some stretches to get the kinks out of my lower back.

Bozeman stepped off the bus and walked past me.

"Where are you going?" I asked.

Bozeman didn't answer, just pointed ahead of him and kept walking. Ah, the park had bathroom facilities, which were nice. Although we had such amenities on the bus, Bozeman hated emptying the black water tanks with a passion, so we used alternate options whenever we could.

When I heard the gig was at a park, I didn't quite know what to expect. Some parks we've played were really nice, complete with permanent structures and food vendors. Other parks were nothing more than a mowed patch of grass with not so much as a shade tree to camp under. This park was on the nicer side. Beyond the restrooms Bozeman was making a beeline for was what looked to be an Olympic-sized swimming pool. That made me hope the restroom included a shower of some sort. About a hundred yards south of the pool, there was a small amphitheater, complete with a covered stage, and I assumed that was where the concert would take place. Overall, the venue pleased me.

I got back on the bus and walked to my room, which was at the rear of the bus. It was past the small kitchen/living area combo, Bozeman's bedroom, the phone booth-sized bathroom, and the room we used to store our gear. On my bed was a small pile of pillows. I usually stacked them with care, but they must have succumbed to the jostle of the potholes because two out of four of them were on the floor. My tuxedo cat, Gibson, seemed unfazed and was in the middle of the bed giving himself a bath when I entered. He spotted me, gave out a half-meow, and returned to work on his tail. I saw he was fine, so I gave him a couple of pets, then let him be.

Outside the bus, I opened the under-bus storage compartment where Merle and Dolly lived. They were both asleep, and it didn't surprise me since, as a skunk and a raccoon, respectively, they were both more active during the nighttime hours. They both slept on old blankets, and I ran a hand beneath Dolly's blanket to see what treasures she had.

Dolly was a three-legged raccoon and loved to bring shiny or interesting things home when she was out gallivanting at night. Every day, I checked her stash and removed anything that could be a danger to either her or her roommate. When I opened my hand, I found a penny and a half-dozen colorful rocks. The penny I kept for the change jar, the rocks I put back where I found them. I don't understand why Dolly has an attraction to rocks, but she always picks up a few every day. When she had too many beneath her blanket, I picked through them and kept the most colorful ones, and the rest I tossed back into the parking lot.

Merle didn't collect stuff except lots of hugs and kisses because he loved being the center of attention. Usually he'd appear around dinner time, would spend the night doing whatever he did, hang out with us during breakfast, then head to bed for the day.

Both of their food dishes were empty, so I removed those, unhooked their mostly empty water bottle, then left them to their dreams.

They were good, so I moved to the rear of the bus to check on my other two friends. Waylon and Willie were a pair of chipmunks who had made a nest in a smaller compartment where a hole had rusted through the compartment door. As I got closer, I could hear them chittering, and they were excited to see me. I pushed aside a bit of chicken wire we used to close the hole when we were in motion and said hello. Usually, chipmunks lived in nests made of leaves, twigs, bark, grass, and sometimes garbage. But Waylon and Willie had top-tier accommodations and lived in nests composed of a holey T-shirt and a pair of socks that Bozeman donated to them.

I held my hand flat, and Willie jumped into my palm and sat still. Once I gave him a scratch between the ears, he jumped to the ground and ran off. Waylon followed, and while they skittered away, I collected their little food and water dishes. I then removed and shook out their bedding and put everything back as I found it.

I took all the bowls to the kitchen and washed and dried them. The water bottle I rinsed out and refilled with a jug of water from the fridge. I was just about ready to give them some food when Bozeman returned.

"Please tell me there's a shower available over there," I said.

"A nice big one. I'm headed back for one right now." Bozeman disappeared into his room. A few minutes later, he came out with a small canvas bag filled with a fresh change of clothes and the sundry items he'd need for a shower.

"I'll head that way too once I'm done feeding the kids. You got your keys?"

"Yeah," Bozeman said as he stepped back off the bus.

I opened the fridge and found some leafy greens for Merle and Dolly to share. For Merle, I picked out a few cherry tomatoes, which were his favorite, and for Dolly, I unpeeled a banana and sliced it into small pieces. The chipmunks got a treat of a handful of trail mix. Before I put it in the bowl, I painstakingly removed the chocolate pieces from it because I was greedy and liked to save those for myself. I was feeling extra-generous and added a small cracker with a dab of peanut butter on it to the mix. They'd be living high on the hog when they got back to the nest.

Merle had half an eye open and watched me as I set out the food and replaced their water bottle. He was still groggy, so he barely moved when I scratched him on the nose between his eyes. Usually, he enjoyed having his belly scratched, but he didn't seem to have enough energy to roll over. I knew how that was. I didn't like to get up sometimes either.

Once my chores were complete, I did just as Bozeman had done and collected everything I needed for the shower. For ease, I slipped out of my jeans and into a pair of sweatpants, and I traded in my socks and sneakers for a pair of flip-flops, then trundled off to the bathhouse. The shower facilities were even nicer than I'd expected. There were a dozen lockers to keep things in, and four individual shower stalls. The one I picked seemed to be almost new. The stainless-steel fixtures gleamed, the tile was immaculate, and although I'd leave on my flip-flops, the floor looked clean. I turned on the water, then stepped out into the main locker area to undress, then grabbed my soap, shampoo, conditioner, and towel, and returned to the shower.

To me, there was nothing better than stepping into a nice, steamy shower. Since we spent so much time on the road, we used our on-bus shower sparingly and didn't dawdle when we did. In here, I could take my sweet time, and could even rinse and repeat, just like the instructions on the shampoo bottle suggested.

I didn't time myself, but I stayed in there long enough to wash the road grunge from my body and sing an entire album's worth of tunes. Although my fingers looked like prunes, I wanted to stay in there even longer. I knew I couldn't, so with a frown and a pout I shut off the water, dried myself off, wrapped the towel tightly around me, and went into the locker room. I was the only one in there, so I took my time getting dressed and then brushing out my hair. As I did so, I looked at myself in the mirror.

"Purple next time. A nice deep purple," I said to my reflection.

My transformation was complete, and I felt relaxed, clean, and ready to take on the world. I looked around to make sure I had everything with me, then walked back to the bus.

Bozeman was already there and had been so for a while. He had set out our favorite lawn chairs next to the bus, and between them was a small cooler. He had a beer in his hand and was reading through a tattered copy of an old Louis L'Amour western. I noticed my guitar was laying across my chair, which was a giant hint that Bozeman expected me to keep my word about playing for him. He watched as I set my shower bag on the bus steps and took up the guitar. I slung the strap over my head, checked the tuning, and broke into a small set of about half the songs I'd already sung in the shower just a few minutes earlier. I thought I sounded pretty good, considering I hadn't played for almost a week.

When I finished, Bozeman nodded at me, then went back to his book. I took my guitar, picked up my shower bag, and headed to my room to stow everything where it belonged. I would've loved to leave things out and deal with them later, but I found that living in such a small space really didn't lend itself to being too much of a slob.

Once I finished, I rejoined Bozeman outside, and he handed me a bottle of lemonade from the cooler. Which I gratefully accepted. I opened the lemonade and had a drink. It wasn't as good as homemade, but it was good enough to be refreshing.

"Are you worried about tomorrow?" I asked.

Bozeman glanced at me over his book, then set it in his lap. "Why would I be?"

"It's got to be a little nerve-wracking for you. Having your friend get picked up by a big label with his career seemingly on the upswing. Yet you and I drive around in this old bus playing in venues just large enough to hold a large bingo tournament."

Bozeman rocked back in his chair and took a swig of his beer. "Not really. I lived that lifestyle for a long time, back before we even met, and I actually prefer what we have. We don't have to worry about promoters or agents or managers. We have control over our lives that he won't have. We play the gigs we want to play, cut albums when we want to, write music when we want to, take a break when we need to. The problem with being a star is you don't have control over anything, from what you eat to how you dress. No, I'm not jealous at all. If anything, I'm sure in a couple of years, Toby will be jealous of me."

"Yeah, but he'll probably be rolling in dough."

Bozeman shrugged. "Maybe. Maybe not. All depends on how ethical the people around him are. You've heard plenty of stories of musicians and actors bilked out of their hard-earned money because of terrible managers or dirty deals, right? There's no way to tell. So, I'm good here. Besides, we seem to be doing just fine."

I nodded in agreement and let it drop. "Any idea on when your friend will be here?"

Bozeman finished his beer, then pulled another from the cooler. "I'd say in about ninety seconds."

I turned and glanced at the road, and headed in our direction was a tour bus that made the same arc Bozeman did and pulled into the spot right next to ours. It was my turn to feel embarrassed. I had bought our old bus from an old musician friend of my mom's. It was a good thirty years old and showed its age sitting next to the shiny new model that pulled up beside us.

It was time for the event to begin.

CHAPTER TWO

The bus rocked a bit after the engine shut down, so I guessed there were more people on it than just two. Five minutes later, the door opened and a tall man with pale skin and shoulder-length dark hair rushed out. He glanced at us and turned and jogged to the restroom.

"Is that your friend? He's kind of rude," I said.

"No, that's not Toby. I have no clue who that is. Here he comes now."

Bozeman stood and watched as the next man from the bus approached. Bozeman offered his hand to shake, but the man took Bozeman into a bear hug and laughed. "Jesse James, it's so good to see you. Man, it's been forever."

The man let Bozeman go and turned his attention to me. "You must be Codi Cassidy." He smiled after he spoke and held out his hand. I offered mine, but rather than a real handshake, he lightly grabbed my fingertips for a second, then released his grip in a hurry. "I'm Toby Madden. It's so nice to meet you. I've heard great things about you."

I smiled back at him. He wasn't a bad-looking man. He was

roughly six feet tall, only a couple inches shorter than Bozeman, and he had light brown hair that had a slight curl, and deep blue eyes. Beneath his shirt, I noticed he had a bit of a beer belly starting, but I imagined he'd work that off pretty fast once he got on tour. "Thank you. And thanks for inviting us to open up for you. It's a real honor."

"Jesse tells me —"

Bozeman interrupted. "Bozeman."

Toby turned around and faced his friend. "Huh?"

"Bozeman. I've told you that like a hundred times. I haven't gone by 'Jesse' in twenty years."

"Why not? Jesse James is a cool name."

"It got old when every person I met either made a stupid crack about me robbing a train, or put their hands in the air, expecting me to take their wallet. Honestly, I don't know what my parents were thinking when they named me that. Since I'm from Montana, most people started calling me Bozeman anyway, so the name stuck."

Toby looked at me. "So, Codi, my guess is that you're from Wyoming?"

I shook my head. "Close. I'm originally from Denver. My parents named me after my mom's favorite aunt."

Toby didn't know what to do with that information, so he smiled for a moment. I saw a bit of relief pass over his face when he noticed a couple of women get off the bus.

"Hey, meet some of the band," he said to us and turned and yelled for the women. "Girls, come over here and meet these folks."

As they approached, I could tell they certainly weren't girls, which was a term that pricked at my brain like an ice cube on an exposed tooth cavity.

"Meet Frannie Love, she plays bass."

The first woman stepped forward and extended her hand. She was, in a word, gorgeous. She was as tall as Toby, had beautiful, tanned skin, mid-length wavy blond hair, and emerald green eyes. I suspected Bozeman was already in love and was currently visualizing his happily ever after with her.

"It's Fran. I'm pleased to know you."

The second woman took my hand without waiting for an introduction. "I'm Laurel Preston. I play the fiddle and sing background vocals."

Laurel was a little more my size. She looked to be about five foot two, had a head of curly red hair, and small gray eyes. Her hand was warm, although somewhat sweaty in mine, and she lingered for a moment longer than was the norm.

I let go of her hand, and as I stood, I discreetly wiped my hand on my jeans. "It's good to meet both of you. I'd love to have a bassist and a fiddler in my band. Why don't you come over and join me? I'll trade the two of you for Bozeman, and we could be the next great all-female trio."

The group laughed, then out of the blue, Laurel winked at me. "I'd be all for that," she whispered, which generated another round of laughter.

The man who ran for the restrooms strolled back and joined the group. Of all of them, he looked the most out of place. He stood about five-ten, had pale skin, long hair that I could tell was dyed black, and dark brown eyes. I pegged him at being in his mid-twenties, a good ten years behind everyone else. He dressed head to toe in black but looked nothing like a Johnny Cash lover.

Toby motioned toward the man. "Here's the newest edition to our group. Gabe Galvin. He's my new drummer."

"Nice to meet you." I stuck out my hand, but Gabe simply looked at it like he'd never seen one before. I let my arm fall back to my side. Without a word, Gabe left and got back on the bus.

"Sorry about that. Gabe's having trouble transitioning into our band. He used to play with a death metal group out of L.A., but he was looking for a change, and my agent asked me to bring him on as a favor. My previous drummer called it quits on me, so I needed one in a hurry and said yes."

I doubted that was the case, but since it wasn't my band, it wasn't my business, either.

Toby looked around the area. "That's all my people. Where are yours?"

I sat back down in the chair. I never liked to just stand around and talk. It always felt awkward to me. "Don't have anyone else. It's just the two of us."

Fran looked confused, so I explained. "I have backing tracks for everything else on the computer. Drums, piano, bass, whatever we need."

Laurel frowned. "It's not the same."

"I know, but we're a small-time operation, and it works for us, and to some extent, gives us more flexibility. Although, I'm thinking of adding a fiddle player." I threw Laurel an exaggerated wink.

Laurel giggled and grabbed Fran's arm. "Come on, I need to go use the facilities. See y'all later." Laurel and Fran turned and headed toward the restrooms.

I watched as the women literally skipped away, and the image changed when a short, rotund man stepped into view. Unlike the rest of us, he dressed in tan slacks rather than blue jeans, and a button-down dress shirt rather than the casual T-shirts everyone else wore. He came forward and presented Bozeman with his business card. Bozeman glanced at it without really reading it, then shoved it between the pages of his book. I knew it was bad business card etiquette, and I hoped it wouldn't offend the man, even though he offended me by ignoring me completely.

"Cody Cassidy, I presume," the man said to Bozeman.

"No. Over here. I'm Codi Cassidy. With an I, not a Y, like what's written on the bus you're standing next to."

The man glanced at me, swiveled his head to read the side of the bus, then settled his eyes back on me. His cheeks were reddening, which meant I had embarrassed him, which I didn't mind since he was the one with the bad assumptions to begin with.

"My apologies, Ms. Cassidy." He started over and handed me a business card, which I shoved right into my back pocket without reading.

"Please. Call me Codi."

"Codi. Fine. Thank you. My name is Russell Davidson. I'm Toby's manager and promoter."

I glanced at Toby. He caught my gaze and rolled his eyes in return. "I'll bet you are."

Russell did his best to recover, stood straighter, and donned the smile of a businessperson looking to make a deal. "May I ask who your representation is, and if you're happy with their services?"

Behind Russell, I saw Toby's chin drop to his chest. He shook his head and took several steps backward to exclude himself from the conversation.

I grinned at Russell. I could play the game too. "Tell me, Russell, how much do you charge?"

"Twenty-three percent."

I exhaled. "You must be good. I thought the typical ceiling was only twenty percent."

Russell subconsciously fiddled with one of his shirt's buttons. "Yes, I believe in going well above and beyond in my service."

"What's your contract length?" I asked.

"Three years," he said without pause.

At that, I sent up an eyebrow. "Twenty-three percent for three years? What if I don't make any money over that time?"

"Well, I take my percentage off the top, of course."

I looked over and saw Bozeman glaring at me so hard it would give me a headache if I kept up the eye contact, so I broke away.

"And what would I get for your services?"

"I'd line up performances, take care of advertising, social media, accounting, taxes, all that sort of thing. Of course, I handle all the business operations, so you're free to concentrate on your performances."

"I see. To answer your original question, we're represented by CB Management, dis-incorporated."

Russell shook his head. "I've never heard of them."

I grinned. "You just met them. I'm the C of CB, and Bozeman over there is the other half of the outfit, and yes, I'm happy with our services."

Russell glanced over at Bozeman, who returned his acknowledgment with a tip of his beer bottle.

Russell looked back at me. "Surely you can't do all that work yourself. You're only a… musician."

I stood, wondering what the word was he originally wanted to use, and felt pretty confident that it was *woman*. I took a step toward him, and although I was a good four inches shorter and a hundred-plus pounds lighter than he was, he yielded the ground to me and stepped back.

"Only a musician? Do you mean I can write songs and learn melodies, but somehow, I'm too stupid to run a business? For your information, I do the bookings, and we have gigs for forty-eight weeks a year. I do the promotion, I run the social media." I threw a thumb in Bozeman's direction. "This hunk over here does the accounting and makes sure we pay the bills, and we hire out a person to do the taxes. We can do everything you can do, and do it better, because we know how to run the business the way it best suits us. So, no. We don't need or want your three-year contract, and certainly not for twenty-three percent." I paused for a moment, let the moment pass, and gave the sweetest smile I could before I put a bit of country twang in my words. "But thank you kindly, sir, for the offer."

I retook my seat.

Russell turned to Toby and was about to say something when Toby stopped him and clapped him on the back. "I'll tell you what, Russell, why don't you quit while you're behind, and run onto the bus and check e-mails or something?"

Russell looked at Toby for a moment, then stomped off in a huff.

Toby sat on the bus steps. "Sorry about that. He can be a bit of a pill to swallow."

Bozeman extracted a beer from the cooler, twisted off the cap, and passed it to Toby. "How did you find that guy?"

Toby drank, emitted a soft burp, and shrugged. "Excuse me. Yeah, the record company saddled him with us. I didn't really have a say in the matter. Once you get past the snark and bluster, he's not that bad."

"Does he really save all that work for you?" I asked.

Toby's facial expression told me everything. "Like I said, he came included in our contract. To be honest, though, we were getting by fine without him. Laurel and Fran handled most of the promotion stuff, and to an extent, still do. The studio hooked us up with an accountant, so Russell primarily sets up the gigs, then acts as the manager once we get on site and need the stage set up."

I chuckled. "Sounds like a great deal to benefit him. Really doesn't add up to twenty-three percent in my mind."

"Codi, don't move." Toby whispered.

"What? Why?"

"There's a mouse right by your foot."

I leaned over and looked, despite the warning. It was Willie. I bent over and held out my hand. Willie climbed into my palm, then sat down, and I sat back in my chair. "This isn't a mouse. It's Willie. He's a chipmunk. Haven't you ever seen a chipmunk before?"

Toby leaned in closer. "Sorry, I'm not wearing my glasses. Looked like a mouse to me. Why are you holding a chipmunk?"

At that moment, Willie twitched, expelled a nut from his cheek, and dropped it into my hand next to him.

"Apparently, he thought I needed a snack."

Bozeman and Toby both laughed.

"We have two chipmunks. Waylon is probably running around here somewhere, or he returned to his nest. It's getting pretty late in the day. Thanks for the nut, Willie, but you can have it."

I picked up the nut and held it out for Willie. He grabbed it with his cute little chipmunk paws and shoved it back into his cheek. He started turning in circles, which was chipmunk talk for putting him down, so I lowered my hand to the ground, and he ran off to the bus.

"That's the strangest thing I think I've ever seen," Toby said.

I smiled as I thought of Merle and Dolly. "Trust me, I can show you stranger."

"No, that's okay. I'll pass."

Bozeman got up and shifted his chair so he could more easily see his friend. "Tell me about the new album."

Toby took a swig, and I took that as he meant to think about it for a moment. "Well, I think you'll like it. It's not really the old-time country, but not like the pop-inspired country of today either. There's plenty of guitars and fiddle, but it doesn't sound like a rock album, if you know what I mean."

Bozeman nodded. I got the gist as well. Lots of country stars out there played music that would transcend past the traditional country fan to more of a broad base.

"What about the release party tomorrow night? What are you expecting?" I asked.

"Guest list is invitation only, mostly to friends and family, a couple hundred people. I'm originally from here, so I wanted to do something special for the home folk. Of course, it's a public park, so I suspect the crowd may get to twice as large with people who just show up, and I'm good with that. Gates, as they are, open at six, party starts at seven."

"What about amenities?"

"There'll be a couple of food trucks here. The record company's sending them over. They're also sending out a crew in the morning to take care of the sound system and lighting, so y'all won't need to worry about that. If you have any special equipment you want, make sure you take it over when they get here. Russell will be on hand to supervise everything, so go to him for anything you need."

I wanted to get down to the brass tacks, primarily, what they expected from Bozeman and I. "What about us? How long should our set be?"

"County law says we need to be shut down by eleven, so you can play for an hour or an hour and a half if you want to. Do you got enough material to cover that?"

I nodded. "Of course. What do you think, Boze?"

Bozeman ciphered it in his head. "Probably an hour at most will be good. We should do a fifty-minute set and come out for an encore."

It sounded like a good plan to me.

"Do you have merch to sell?" Toby asked.

"Yeah, but nothing too wild. CDs, signed photos, T-shirts, stuff like that. Can we set up a table?"

"For sure. If you're good with it, Fran and Laurel can run it for you while you're onstage, and a bit after until you can take over. You can trust them, and they're pretty good salespeople. They could sell anything to anyone, and like I said, they're both trustworthy, so you don't have to worry about the till."

"Sounds good. Appreciate the favor," Bozeman said.

"Good, then maybe you two could do one for me in return. Come on up and join me and the band for our encore."

I looked at Bozeman, who seemed fine with it. Usually when we were on a bill with other acts, we'd usually catch anyone playing before us, then stay for most of the act following us, then head back to the bus. Neither one of us was big on traditional after parties.

"We can do that. What's the song?"

"It's an original. Real easy standard three chord progression, you'll pick it up pretty fast. We'll practice it at sound check tomorrow at four. Does that work?"

"Sure thing." It didn't bother me. We had nowhere else to be, and all day to travel the couple hundred yards to the stage.

Fran walked up, put her hands on her hips, and leaned in toward Toby. "Are you going to fire up the grill, or are you going to sit here chatting all night? Come on, your crew is hungry." She grabbed Toby's arm and forced him to his feet.

"Okay, okay, I'm coming. Would you two like to join us? Dinner is nothing fancy, just burgers, beans, potato salad, and the like, but you're welcome. We've got plenty of food."

I turned to Bozeman. "What do we have on the menu for tonight's feast?"

He thought for a moment. "Well, you can have your choice of canned beef stew or a peanut butter and jelly sandwich."

I looked back at Toby and Fran, who still had a tight hold on his arm. "We'll be right over."

After Toby and Fran left, Bozeman and I cleaned up our little area and while Bozeman carried the cooler onto the bus, I checked on Dolly and Merle. Although it wouldn't be dark for another hour, they were both stirring from their naps. I noticed the banana and tomato treats were already gone, and I took the time to give them both head and belly scratches. I left the door open so they could roam when they wanted to, and I got on the bus to wash my hands and grab a light jacket since I usually get a chill once the sun sets.

A few minutes later, Bozeman and I strode over to Toby's bus. The way Fran talked about the grill, I expected one of those small charcoal things that only fit a couple of burgers at a time. It amazed me to see that the bus came with a full outdoor kitchen.

Toby had on a chef's hat and an apron that said 'kiss the cook', and he was working a flat top grill that easily held eight hamburgers. Next to that was a pan filled with onions and mushrooms, and another burner held a pot of baked beans. A portable picnic table large enough for ten people was set up, and Fran and Gabe were setting the table. Laurel stepped off the bus carrying a tray of hamburger buns and a basket filled with a bottle of ketchup, at least four types of mustard, salt and pepper, relish, and other condiments.

Toby impressed me with his prowess in the kitchen. "You got that going quickly. You just left us like ten minutes ago."

Toby looked up and smiled at me. "Yeah, well, we all work as a unit. Gabe got everything started out here while the girls prepped all the food. Russell's still in there making some coleslaw."

"He can cook too? Besides all the other duties he performs?"

Laurel laughed at me. "I wouldn't call it cooking. It's mostly pre-made. He just has to dump everything into a bowl and stir. The rule is for everyone to eat, everyone has to contribute to the meal."

"That sounds great, but who do you decide who does the dishes?"

"That's easy," Toby said. "If no one volunteers, we play one round of Texas hold'em, and the two weakest hands share the cleanup duties."

Laurel elbowed me in the ribs. "That usually means it's Gabe and Russell. Neither one is lucky at cards."

I shrugged. "Well, that only means they must be lucky at love."

Laurel wrinkled her nose at the prospect. "Eww. So gross, Codi. Why don't y'all grab a drink over at the fridge there and take a seat?"

Bozeman needed no further invitation, so he went and came back with a beer for himself and a bottle of water for me. We both found seats and Laurel, Fran, and Gabe joined us. Toby came over and dropped off a bowl holding the onion and mushroom mixture, and another containing the baked beans, then went back to the grill. Russell appeared with his coleslaw and found a seat, and then Toby returned with a platter of hamburgers.

I waited, wondering if someone was going to say grace or something. Instead, Toby cleared his throat and picked up his glass. "A toast to our friends, Codi and Bozeman." We all clinked glasses together and dug into our evening meal.

CHAPTER THREE

The next morning at eight on the dot, I was about to step off the bus when I received a knock on the door. When I opened it, I looked out and noticed Laurel standing there with a box in her hands.

"Good morning. Would you like a donut?" She smiled at me as she lifted the small box as if paying tribute.

It was a gracious gesture, offering someone you just met a donut, and I was more than happy to take her up on the offer. "Only if you'll have one with me. Come on in."

I stepped back into the common area, and Laurel followed me. I pointed to the small bench table. "Have a seat. Would you like some coffee or something?"

Laurel placed the box on the table and slid into the seat. "You won't believe this, but I can't stand coffee. Tea or juice or even a can of cola would be fine."

I moved to the refrigerator to determine what we had in stock. There was a pitcher of what I remembered to be orange juice, but when I picked it up, I realized one of us had put it back in the fridge empty. In our world, that wasn't considered a spiteful act. It usually meant that either Dolly or Merle was aboard, and we didn't want them getting into something they shouldn't. Sometimes our fridge contained more empty, dirty containers than actual food. Until, at last, one of us broke down and did the dishes, or needed room after a grocery run. No luck, so I stepped over to the pantry.

"I've got Diet Dr. Pepper or water I can offer you. Got a preference?"

"I'll take the Dr. Pepper," Laurel said.

"It's in a can. Would you like a glass, or ice?" I should have checked if we had ice before I offered her some.

"Nah. I can take it right out of the can."

I grabbed a couple of cans and some napkins and sat at the table.

Laurel took a can, wiped the top off with a napkin, popped it open, and took a sip. "Thanks. This is great. Have a donut."

She pushed the box toward me, and I flipped the lid open. There were four donuts inside, and I immediately gravitated to the Boston Creme, like a shark going after an injured fish. As graceful as a giraffe wearing oven mitts, I picked it from the box and took a bite. I loved the taste of chocolate on my lips and the explosion of pastry creme onto my tongue.

"Those are my favorite, too." Laurel reached into the box and extracted what looked to be a blueberry cake donut.

As we ate in silence, I looked Laurel over. When I met her, she was standing next to Fran, who, because she resembled a Greek goddess, took all the attention. But as I looked at Laurel as she sat by herself, I discovered she could more than hold her own. Today she had her fiery red hair pulled back in a bun, and her complexion was flawless, except for a small mole on her neck just below her right ear. She wore no makeup that I could tell, and she was what my mom would refer to as a classic beauty. Even though she dressed in dark blue sweatpants and a gray T-shirt with an alien on the front.

I finished my donut, wiped my mouth and fingers with a napkin, and pointed at her shirt. "You believe in aliens?"

Laurel gave me a crooked smile, brushed her donut crumbs into her hand, and placed them atop her napkin. "You'll probably think I'm a kook, but yes."

"Why?" I hoped the question didn't sound as rude out loud as it did in my head. "Sorry, I'm just curious."

Laurel smiled at me. "No problem. For me, it's just math. Even within the Milky Way, there are probably forty or fifty billion planets that may support life as we recognize it. Even if there was a one percent chance of life on those planets, that would still be forty million populated worlds out there."

I nodded. The numbers made sense to me. "Then why didn't the little green people contact us yet?"

"Good question, and my answer is, think about it. Let's say there is life on other planets. You can't assume that those life forms are in the same advanced stage we are, right? I mean, it took humans, what? Six or seven million years to evolve to where we are now? There might be millions of life forms out there that haven't reached our stage of maturity yet, still discovering fire and such. Or lifeforms that aren't as advanced technologically to cross the stars."

Made sense to me. "Do you think we'll ever get visited by aliens?"

She winked at me. "Who's saying we haven't been? Who's saying the whole human race isn't an offshoot of some civilization from some faraway planet?"

We sat in silence for a moment, eyes locked. I broke it first. "It's way too early to be having this conversation."

"So, where's Bozeman this morning?" Laurel asked.

"If he's not on the bus, and he wasn't outside, he is in the shower or out for a run."

A sly smile crossed Laurel's face. "If I may be so bold to ask, what's the deal with you two?"

I knew what she meant by that. It was the same question in one form or another that I got asked almost every time I met a new group of people.

"There's nothing going on there. We're just business partners."

"Oh. I see."

I wondered if she did. It seemed the concept of two people living on a bus and traveling around the country playing music together, yet not being romantically involved, was over many people's heads. Most people didn't believe me. After all, Bozeman's a good-looking guy. Tall, dark, and handsome with the six-pack abs and flashy smile, like he just stepped out of a cheesy romance novel, but there were zero sparks for either of us. We were friends and colleagues, and that was the extent of it.

"Honest. Ask him out if you want to," I said.

Laurel tilted her head and tugged at the neck of her T-shirt. "No, he's not really my type. He'd probably find Fran more attractive, anyway. Everyone always does."

A second later, Laurel shrieked and pulled her legs up onto the bench seat. She tried to speak, but couldn't, and instead pointed at the floor behind me.

"What?" I turned around and saw Dolly sitting on the floor, her whiskers twitching in our direction. I bent over, Dolly came forward, and I swooped her up in my arms. "I must have left the door open. This is Dolly."

Laurel determined she wasn't in danger, and returned her feet to the floor. To my surprise, she leaned toward Dolly and held out a hand. "She's a raccoon! Can I pet her?"

"Sure," I said and held Dolly out so Laurel could reach her better.

Laurel moved her fingers closer and Dolly reciprocated by wrapping her tiny human-like hand around Laurel's finger. It looked like they were shaking hands.

"Give her a scratch on her nose there between the eyes, and

she'll be your friend forever."

Laurel did as I suggested, and Dolly squirmed in my grip until I let her go. She walked across the table and plopped down in front of Laurel.

"She's so cute. Can I give her a donut?"

"Maybe. What do you have left in the box?"

"Another blueberry cake, and a jelly filled."

"Go with the blueberry. And only half, okay?"

Laurel nodded, opened the box, pulled the donut in half, and closed the box. She broke the donut into smaller chunks and offered one to Dolly. Dolly, who was never shy when being offered food, took it in her paws and nibbled away at it.

"She's adorable. Where did you get her?"

"I got her from a veterinarian as a kit. Someone had found her and brought her in because of her leg. She was born without a back leg."

Laurel held the donut up in the air, so Dolly had to reach for it. When Dolly extended her body, her birth defect became apparent. "That's amazing. Okay, girl, last chunk." Laurel fed the remains of the donut to Dolly.

After she ate the last bite, Dolly jumped from the table to the seat next to me, and then to the floor. She took a couple of steps, then groomed herself, much like a cat would.

"If you think that's amazing, grab that other half of that donut and follow me," I said.

Laurel grabbed the donut and trailed me outside. We stopped by the door, and I bent over and saw that Merle was home and still awake, which was a good thing. He had a tendency to be grumpy if anyone woke him, a trait we shared. I reached into the cubbyhole and brought him out.

"This is Merle," I said.

Laurel's jaw dropped in surprise. I couldn't judge what was going through her mind, and she didn't speak for a good twenty seconds. "Can I hold him?"

"Sure. Sit down."

Laurel sat in Bozeman's lawn chair, and I put Merle on her lap. "He like belly rubs, tomatoes, and blueberry donuts."

Merle did a quick circle in Laurel's lap, determined she wasn't a threat, and laid down on his side. Laurel broke off a chunk of donut and offered it to him. "Where did you get a skunk?"

"Picked him up the same place I got Dolly."

"You're too much, Codi. Any other surprises around here?"

I shook my head. "No. Just a cat and a couple of chipmunks. How is it you're so good with animals?"

Laurel broke off more donut. Merle was enjoying his morning snack, or rather, since he was mostly nocturnal, his bedtime snack. "I grew up on a farm. I've been an animal lover since I was a little girl. When I was young, I wanted to be a vet or work in a zoo."

"And you ended up playing fiddle in a country band?"

Laurel gave me a smile with a hint of sadness behind it. "Yeah. You know, life impedes your plans sometimes, right?"

I nodded in agreement. I knew how that went.

"What are you three up to?"

I turned and saw Bozeman. I hadn't even detected his approach, and usually I was well aware of my surroundings. He dressed in sweatpants and a T-shirt and was carrying his shower bag, and his hair was wet.

"I'm just introducing Laurel to the kids."

Bozeman nodded at Laurel. She nodded back, and he got back on the bus. As she fed the last of the donut to Merle, I saw Dolly stepping off the bus. Merle noticed her as well, shifted in Laurel's lap, and jumped to the ground. From there, they went into their compartment.

"It's bedtime for them," I explained.

Laurel frowned. "Is it safe for them to live in a storage compartment under the bus like that?"

"Sure. They prefer it over living on the bus since it's more like they're used to in the wild. Bozeman even fixed it up, so it's well-ventilated, heated in the winter, and cooled in the summer. In short, whatever the temperature is on the bus, it's the same temperature in their little apartment."

"And you let them run free?" Laurel asked.

"Sure. They always know where home is. We only lock them up when we're on the road, so no one falls off the bus. We wouldn't want that to happen."

"This is too much. Hey, I've got to get going. See you later, right?"

"Of course, we'll be here all day."

At quarter to four, Bozeman and I walked over to the amphitheater, ready for the sound check. I lugged my favorite Martin guitar with me while Bozeman pulled a folding wagon holding his pedal board and his Gibson. As we got closer, I could see a crew had been hard at work setting up for the event. There was a soundboard set up, a professional lighting rig over the stage, and a literal tower of large black speakers and amps. From the looks of it, people wouldn't need to come to the park to hear the concert. They'd be able to enjoy it from their house if they lived anywhere within a three-mile radius.

Russell appeared from out of nowhere and stopped us from going any farther. "Hold up here. Toby's going to do a short sound check, then I'll get you settled."

Although the amphitheater had paved aisles running from the top of the hill to the stage, it didn't have traditional seats. Instead, the seating area looked like an agricultural terrace and had eighteen-inch-high steps set into the hill. At the end of each step was a brick wall, about twelve inches wide, topped with a capstone for seating. Bozeman angled his wagon into the step so it wouldn't roll to the stage and sat. I followed suit, setting my guitar case at my feet.

I looked at Russell. "What's the plan?"

"Toby's band will play though four or five songs until the sound engineer is happy. If we're lucky. Then you two can set up and do a quick check, and then y'all will run through Toby's encore."

"Why if we're lucky?"

Russell shrugged. "Sometimes Toby gets into a snit with the sound guys and plays the same song repeatedly until he's happy. It drives everyone nuts. The engineers, the band, me, but he insists on doing it."

At that moment, Gabe appeared on stage, followed by Fran and Laurel. He ran through his drum kit to make sure he liked the positioning of the equipment while the women checked the tuning on their respective instruments. Gabe looked into the audience at Russell. Russell checked the venue to make sure everyone was in place, then gave Gabe the thumbs up. Gabe clacked his sticks together, then began a beat. A few seconds later, Toby strolled out on stage, and the sound check began.

At first, it was a bumpy beginning to get the sound levels correct for the venue. Once the technicians had the sound figured out, the band settled into a short set to get warmed up. I was enjoying the music when I heard a gruff voice behind Bozeman.

"Excuse me, sir. Could you remove that ugly hat?"

Bozeman and I both turned, and Bozeman jumped to his feet. "Well, I'll be. Tommy Skye! How are you, man?" Bozeman held out his hand and Tommy shook it.

"Been better. Codi, I assume. Nice to meet you."

I offered my hand.

"Tommy Skye is one of the best guitar players in the business. What are you doing down here? I thought you were with the band."

Tommy looked at the stage, then back at Bozeman. "Nah, we've had a falling out. I'm not with them anymore."

"Got a new gig?" Bozeman asked.

Tommy sniffed, produced a ragged tissue from his pocket

like a magician, and rubbed his nose. "No. I haven't played in a while."

Bozeman nodded. "Well, it's good to see you. You're looking good."

Bozeman and I must have a different opinion of what good looks like, because the man didn't look good to me at all. He was five-eight, and I could tell he'd lost a lot of weight recently based on how much tongue hung from his belt loop. He wore a buttoned denim jacket that looked to be three sizes too big for him, and his gaunt appearance made him look like a living skeleton. I wondered if the falling out he mentioned had anything to do with illegal narcotics.

Russell whistled at us from the stage and waved us over. I hadn't noticed Toby's band was done with their check. We said our goodbyes to Tommy and climbed to the stage where Bozeman set up his pedal board, and I removed my guitar from the case and gave it a quick tuning. We took our positions with me out front and center and Bozeman just a step behind and a pace to my left. Together, we worked through two songs until I got the signal from the sound engineer that we were ready.

When we finished, Toby's band joined us on stage, and Toby explained his idea for the encore. The first song was an old Willie Nelson standard I could play in my sleep, and probably had at one time or another. The last song we'd sing was the first released single of the new album.

"Just watch the monitor there for the lyrics and chord changes," Toby instructed. "We'll run through it two or three times, so you get the feel."

I looked down near the front of the stage and noticed the black box I thought was an amplifier was actually a video monitor that looked like an amp. From the audience side, it would look like a piece of audio equipment, and they wouldn't be able to tell it fed the musicians the lyrics and chord progressions. The band started, and I watched the monitor as they played through it once so we could hear it. Overall, it was a nice, albeit old-fashioned country ballad about a cowboy alone on the plains, reminiscing about a lost love. The tune was catchy, and the lyrics told such a poignant story. I knew it had the makings of a gold, if not platinum, record.

Russell appeared from the wings and gave us each a copy of the sheet music to *Dancing Teardrops*, the song we'd just played.

I glanced over at Bozeman, and he looked unhappy. He wore a snarl on his face, and his cheeks were turning red. The paper he clenched in his fist. My first thought was he was suffering a seizure. "Boze? Are you okay?"

Bozeman shook his head, jumped from the stage, and ran up the hill. Everyone had gone silent behind me, and I turned to see all the inquisitive faces staring at me. "Um. He had a thing. I'd better go check on him. Excuse me."

I stepped onto the bus and noticed two things. Bozeman had crumpled the sheet music into a ball, and the door to our equipment storage room was open. Since the door opened toward me, I couldn't look in, but I heard Bozeman rummaging around for something.

"Bozeman? You okay in there?"

Bozeman grunted, like he had just lifted something heavy. "Yeah, I found what I'm looking for. Be out in a second."

I made my way back to the table and sat. A few seconds later, the door closed, and Bozeman approached with a cardboard banker's box I'd never seen before.

"It has to be in here." Bozeman opened the box, and I saw it stuffed with notebooks and random sheets of loose-leaf paper. He grabbed a handful of notebooks, set them on the table, and pushed them my way. "Here. Check the inside cover for dates and pull out anything from ten or eleven years ago."

While Bozeman checked the loose papers, I did as he asked. In the end, I had set aside two notebooks from that timeframe.

Bozeman placed the box on the floor and threw all but the two notebooks into the box. He grabbed one notebook and slid the other over to me. "Okay, now go through and see if you recognize anything familiar."

I was confused. "Familiar how?"

Bozeman grabbed the paper ball, smoothed it out, and handed it to me. "Familiar like this."

I opened the notebook and scanned through the pages. I knew Bozeman was a songwriter, but I didn't know he was so prolific. Every page I turned offered a new page of handwritten lyrics with chords or notes penciled in the margins. I checked the notebook's cover, and it said it held eighty pages. Assuming all the pages were there, and each song covered two pages, Bozeman had at least forty songs in this notebook alone. I continued to turn pages until something finally caught my eye. I compared the notebook to the sheet music and turned it around.

"Is this what you're looking for?"

Bozeman nodded. "That's it exactly."

Bozeman took a minute to compare the notebook to the sheet music. "He changed the title, but the music and lyrics match. I thought that song sounded familiar, and now I know why. He stole it from me, that son of a—"

Without continuing his sentence, Bozeman grabbed the notebook and music and raced from the bus. I got up immediately, but by the time I left the bus, Bozeman was already out of sight. Since there was such a height difference between us, and he was a runner and I wasn't, there was no way to keep up with him. By the time I reached the stage, Bozeman was already there and on top of Toby.

"You stole my song!" Bozeman screamed as he threw wild punches at Toby. Although Bozeman had Toby trapped under his gigantic frame, Toby wrapped his arms around his head. Most of Bozeman's manic punches landed with no actual harm.

I stepped forward and grabbed Bozeman's arm. "Help me,"

I implored the others standing around me. They looked like statues, but finally Gabe came and helped me pull Bozeman off of Toby.

"That's enough," I ordered. "Back off, Bozeman."

Gabe helped Toby to his feet. Toby looked ruffled and had a tiny cut on his chin that was barely bleeding, but he didn't look bad at all. I'd seen worse injuries at a post-Thanksgiving sale at a local big box store.

Bozeman's chest heaved as he breathed, and he stuck his finger out at Toby. "I ought to hang you, you thief."

A tense cloud passed over the stage. I didn't know how this stalemate would end. Of course, being the smallest-stature person around, I grabbed Bozeman's arm and pulled him toward the stage stairs. "Come on, cowboy, let's go take a break."

CHAPTER FOUR

I held on to Bozeman and led him all the way back to the bus. To his credit, he never once tried to pull away, even though he could have done so without expending a single calorie's worth of energy. Instead, he trudged along like a zombie.

When we got to the bus, I sat him down in his chair and stood over him like a scolding mother. "I can't believe you did that! He could cancel our gig tonight and sue you for assault, or get you arrested! Are you out of your mind?"

Bozeman threw the puppy-dog-eyes look my way, and I knew I couldn't stay mad at him for long, especially since I wasn't good at anger to begin with. To show him I remained upset, I crossed my arms and sat down with a huff.

"He's not going to call the cops, and he's certainly not going to sue me," Bozeman said.

"How can you be so sure?"

"Because. It will cause him a lot more trouble when it gets out that Toby poached someone else's song, and I sue him for copyright infringement. The record company will drop him like a hot rock."

I picked up the sheet music from the ground where

Bozeman dropped it and checked the citation. It claimed the music and lyrics came directly from the head of Toby Madden. "Maybe it was a mistake. If you talked to him, perhaps he'd change it to give you the writing credit. Then everybody wins, right?"

"That's not going to happen in a billion years. Once it gets around that he stole my song, I'm sure any writer who has ever known him is going to scour Toby's back catalog to check if he stole anyone else's work. And for sure, he won't want to part with any of the royalties he'd have to give up."

"You're not even going to talk to him?" I asked, hoping he'd at least apologize.

Bozeman stood. "What I'm going to do is go for a nice, long walk. I'll be back by six-thirty at the latest."

I watched as Bozeman skulked off in the opposite direction of the stage, so I hoped he wouldn't circle back and cause any more trouble. Conflicted, I felt trapped between going after him and letting him blow off the steam. I opted for the latter.

Instead, I wanted to find Toby and ask if we were still the opening act or if we should get our gear and leave. As I passed his bus, I noticed him headed in my direction, so I stopped and waited for him. The cut on his face had already stopped bleeding, and although his clothes looked wrinkled from the tussle, he didn't look like he'd been in a fight. He saw me, slowed his gait for a few seconds, reconsidered and sped up again and stopped a foot from me.

Toby crossed his arms and tipped his chin up. "Did you come to apologize for him?"

I shook my head. "No. Bozeman's a big boy. That's up to him to do. What I need to find out is if we're still good to open tonight."

Toby glared at me for a moment, then dropped his posture. "Nice and candid. I appreciate that. If I had anyone else on the bill, I'd call the cops and have you removed from the park, but since it's just the two of us, I'm going to let it go. My fans are expecting you, and I still want you to perform. However, the minute your set is done, I'd like you to be gone. No merch, no shared encore. Get on this..." Toby glanced at my old bus and pointed to it. "...machine and go."

I didn't like the deal, but since I had no other options, I nodded. "Yeah, okay. Can I ask you one question, though? Did you steal his song?"

Toby glared into my eyes. I expected him to scream a denial at me, but he turned for his bus without uttering so much as a syllable.

"I'll take that as a yes," I whispered to myself.

He stopped in mid-stride, as if to return, then kept walking. "Did he fire you?"

It was my turn to be startled. I jumped when I heard the voice, then looked behind me. It was Laurel. I hadn't seen or detected her approach, so I assumed she learned how to teleport, or at the very least, was a ninja.

She smiled at me. "Sorry. I didn't mean to scare you. Are you still playing tonight?"

"Yes. But we need to leave right after our set, and we can't sell merch."

"Good. I have all your albums," she said. Laurel smiled. "I'm a big fan."

I blushed. During meet-and-greets I heard those words often, but when a fellow musician said them, it just hit differently. "Thanks. I appreciate that."

"And don't worry about the merch. Toby told me and Fran yesterday about the table, and we'll still run it for you."

My brow creased. "Oh, no, I can't have you getting into any trouble for me."

Laurel waved her hand at me like she shooed away a fly. "What trouble? Toby returned to the bus, and he'll be there until like five minutes before we go on stage. Sometimes he's even late for the set, and once we start to play, he'll spot some blond in the crowd and focus on her all night. I'm sure by the time our gig is half-over, he'll have forgotten about everything."

"Are you sure?"

"I'm positive. So, what do you say?"

I thought about it for a quick minute, then made my decision. "Come on, I'll show you what I have."

I led Laurel to the bus, opened a storage compartment, and brought out the three totes I had filled with various merchandise. We sold signed photos of myself, copies of my CDs, Bozeman's CDs, and, of course, a variety of T-shirts with my pretty face on them. I put the totes on a portable hand truck, and together we wheeled the load to the top of the amphitheater where Russell was busy stocking Toby's merchandise. Although we offered the same stuff, Toby's presentation blew mine away. He had a small, covered portable gazebo for his merch. I had a plastic table. It would do, though. One benefit of having only a couple samples out and working from totes was it only took a few seconds to clean everything up in case of bad weather or a quick getaway.

With Laurel's help, I got things going, and once I showed her the price sheet and how to take credit cards, I excused myself to get dressed for the show. Back on the bus, although I was alone, I could tell Bozeman had been there. The banker's box had disappeared, so I assumed he put it away, and I sensed a hint of his cologne in the air.

I moved to my room and picked out my outfit for the night, which wasn't hard because I had a set wardrobe to choose from. I had three pairs of jeans to choose from. All three were the same brand and style and the only choice I had was color: either black, blue, or dark green. I also had three western shirts, again, same shirt but in different colors. I had a practical system, and everything went together, so I could literally get dressed in the dark and everything in my ensemble would match. Tonight, I went with the black jeans and navy blue checkered shirt. I brushed my teeth, put on my boots, found my hat, and was ready to rock out, or rather, country out.

Ready to go, I was about to leave my bus when I felt a paw on my calf. I looked down, and there was Gibson, working hard to get my attention. I took a step away from him, and he plopped to the ground, expecting belly rubs, which I happily provided while I cooed at him.

"You be a good boy and watch the bus. I'll be back in a couple of hours."

There was still no sight of Bozeman when I got to the stage, but Gabe was there making last-minute adjustments to his kit.

"We really haven't talked. I'm Codi."

Gabe didn't speak.

"Toby told me you're new to the band. Came over from metal, right?"

He looked at me, but again, didn't utter a syllable.

"What's your favorite band? Black Sabbath? Megadeth? Led Zeppelin? Although I think they consider Led Zeppelin classic rock by now. Mine is Metallica."

His eyes widened, so I assumed I had him. "You're familiar with Metallica?"

"Of course, darlin'. My favorite song of theirs is *Enter Sandman*. I love the guitar sound of that song. When I first heard it, I played it repeatedly until my parents begged me to stop. Or rather, the neighbor next door got my parents to make me quit."

To show I learned the tune, I sang a few bars for him.

"Of course, I love *Nothing Else Matters*, too." I sang a bit of that as well to him, and Gabe stood there grinning. I couldn't blame him. Certainly, the boots and hat weren't a typical look to match the music.

"Wow, I'm impressed. I'm surprised you've heard of them. It seems like metal would be outside of your wheelhouse."

"Why? Music's an art and I appreciate it all. Rock, blues, jazz, folk. There's nothing I don't enjoy occasionally. Well, except opera, but I'm sure I'd like that better if I understood Italian. And all those genres borrow from each other. So how you like being in a country band?"

Gabe twirled a drumstick in his hand. "It's so different from what I'm used to. There's not as much energy."

"You mean you miss the younger crowd, more bass guitar and the intensity?"

He tilted his head. "Yeah, kind of."

"I can understand that. What I first started out; my manager would book me into these country bars. You ever been in one?"

Gabe shook his head no.

"Some of them were okay. Nice stage, agreeable sound, respectful crowd, and those weren't so bad at all. Other times, he'd get me a gig at these real rowdy places where they surrounded the stage with chicken wire and the crowd got meaner as the night got longer."

"Why the chicken wire?"

"That was to prevent the band from getting hurt when the locals started throwing beer bottles."

Gabe laughed. "They must have hated you to throw bottles."

"Sometimes. Other times, the locals considered it a sign of respect. Where I came from, respect wasn't throwing glass at people, but different strokes for different folks. And in those places, you could bet that at least one fight would break out during the evening, and we'd just keep on playing like there wasn't a riot happening three feet in front of us. Although one night, a drunkard jumped on my stage, threw a punch at my drummer, and knocked him clean out."

Gabe's eyes widened. "Oh, wow."

"Exactly."

"What did you do?" he asked.

"Well, we took a break long enough for the bouncer to throw out the guy and to wake up the drummer, then we finished the set."

"That's incredible," Gabe said. His ear-to-ear grin told me he liked that story.

"It is. Anyway, I remember there was one night just after we finished a gig in Texas at the roughest place they had ever booked us to play. I was sitting on a barstool, picking bottle glass out of my hair, and my favorite shirt smelled like a brewery. I looked around and wondered how I had gotten there, and how long I'd have to spend playing places like that. It was right then I decided I had enough, so I fired my manager and broke up that band, and vowed to never play in another dive like that again."

I had the eyes from him again, so I could tell I'd lost him. "Long story short, Gabe. Although it was scary, I made a change that, although hard, was better for me in the long run. I'm in a much better place today, mentally and professionally, than had I not gotten out of that comfortable groove I was in. Get it?"

"I think so."

"Take advantage of the opportunity you have now. You can never tell where it will lead, right?"

"That's true."

"What are you talking about?"

I hadn't even noticed Bozeman had joined us. There he was, standing with his guitar slung over his shoulder and pick in hand, ready to play, and when he spoke, it startled me.

I smiled. "Nothing much, just Metallica."

Bozeman rolled his eyes at me. Although I enjoyed a wide range of genres in music, Bozeman was more of a purist. He enjoyed only two types of music: country music produced before 1960, and country music produced after 1960. It was only through my insistence that songs from other genres popped into our set list occasionally.

"It's almost show time," Bozeman said.

I looked out at the sound engineer's booth and spotted the digital clock perched on the table front. A red number ten was visible, so I realized it was only ten minutes before we were on. I did a last-second spot check of my equipment and walked offstage with Bozeman and Gabe into the wings and waited for our introduction.

A few seconds later, Russell appeared at my side. "You ready?"

I looked at Bozeman, and he gave me a nod.

"Yes. We're ready to go," I said.

Russell stepped to center stage and positioned him in front of my microphone. "Ladies and gentlemen, thank you for coming to the show tonight. I know you're all excited about seeing Toby Madden, but before we bring him out, we've got a fantastic act for you. Please help give a warm welcome to Codi Cassidy."

I plastered on a smile, and Bozeman and I took our places on stage. I wouldn't call what we received a warm welcome, more like a smattering of polite golf clapping. That was okay, though, because I knew we weren't the ones the crowd had been hand-selected to see. Tonight, we were only the appetizer for the main entrée.

I ran off a three count, and we hit the opening chord together. In a normal set, Bozeman and I started off with songs that worked well with just us and our two guitars. Once the audience knew it was us behind the magic, I fired up a computer that provided accompanying tracks of different instruments for other songs. I relied on the magic of technology for my pianist, drummer, bassist, fiddler, and any other music we'd need during a set. I also had the program set to where the lights would synchronize with the music. But tonight, I didn't need to worry about running the machine. The engineer was running my computer, and the studio had provided a lighting crew.

We started the set with two of my original songs, and then I slowed it down with a rendition of Dolly Parton's *I Will Always Love You*. I loved that song, not only because it is one of the best songs ever written, but it fits nicely into my vocal range. That was a good one to play for a crowd that didn't know my music. We played a couple more of my songs, then I turned the stage over to Bozeman.

Bozeman stepped forward and played one of his originals, but as he did, I could see that something wasn't quite right with him. He seemed… off, like he wasn't really there. Sure, that was him picking and singing, but I noticed he was really just going through the motions, which was something he never did. Bozeman loved to play live shows, and that joy always translated into an animated performance.

Had this been a rehearsal, I would've stopped the session right there and asked him what the deal was. Since there were a couple hundred people watching us, all I could do was keep up appearances and go on with the show.

Instead of displaying his normal on-stage self, he powered through his song by rote, gave the crowd a thank you, and passed the floor back my way.

I gave a brief introduction of the next song to the crowd. It was more for the benefit of the engineer to let him know he needed to activate the backing tracks on my computer. As I spoke, I looked into the crowd. I spotted Tommy Skye still sitting where we had left him. He saw me looking at him and raised a can of beer and tilted it in my direction. At least he was enjoying the show.

With the music backing tracks, we picked things up a bit, and we intermixed a few popular upbeat country songs into the set that fit in well with my original tunes. That always worked well with a crowd that didn't know my music and kept them up on their feet and cheering and dancing.

I checked the clock on the engineer table and saw it displayed a green three, which means we had time for one more song. I did a quick introduction of my most famous song, *Loving You, Leaving You*, which broke into the top forty of the country chart, and we played that. It was the song that usually got the most applause and cheers, not only because it was an excellent song but also because most people didn't know it had come from me.

Just like that, our part of the show was over. Instead of the polite, golf clap cheers we'd opened to, we received a hearty ovation upon our exit. We'd whipped the crowd up for more music, so I stood satisfied that as the opening act, we had done our job.

Bozeman and I each said thank you to the crowd and took a couple of bows, then headed for the wings.

Russell was there, holding a grin and bottles of water for each of us. "That was great, fabulous! When Toby suggested you as an opening act, I was skeptical, but, boy, you won me over."

"Thank you." I opened the bottle and drank down half the contents.

Bozeman had already emptied his bottle and set it on top of an amp box. "Is there a restroom here, or do I have to use the one by the pool?"

Russell pointed toward a short hallway behind Bozeman. "Follow that hall. Can't miss it."

Bozeman turned and headed in that direction. I wanted to remind him about the merchandise booth, but he was out of sight by the time I thought of it. "When does Toby start?"

Russell stepped around me and looked at the clock. "Just over sixteen minutes. You don't have too much gear. You want the roadies to take it to your bus, or do you want to haul it yourself?"

"Just have them make a small pile and we'll go through it first and make sure we have everything." It was a simple answer. I, along with probably most performing musicians, had found ourselves burned before. It wasn't often intentional, but in the rush to clear the stage, it wasn't uncommon for gear to be misplaced. Not that we had much. I had one guitar and my computer, and Bozeman had two guitars and his pedals, along with our mics and stands, and a handful of assorted cords.

"Hey, I'll be right back." I left Russell and made my way to the merch area at the top of the hill. Laurel was selling a CD to a customer, so I stood aside and waited for the transaction to finish.

When the middle-aged man turned around, he gasped when he noticed me. "Ms. Cassidy, that was such a good show. Would you mind signing this for me?"

I smiled my sweetest smile. "Of course." I stepped around the table and found a small tote that contained all the miscellaneous things I usually needed. From the tote, I grabbed a marker and held out my hand for the CD. The man gave it to me, and I slipped the insert out.

"What's your name, sugar?"

He told me, and I wrote the obligatory "To Tom, Love, Codi Cassidy", and slid the inset back into the case. I passed the CD to him and shook his hand. "Thank you for your support."

I turned back to Laurel. "Thanks for running the booth for me. I really appreciate it. I'll help you pack everything up."

Laurel grinned at me. "No need. There's nothing to pack. You're sold out."

Her words confused me. "Everything?" I pulled the bins from beneath the table and looked inside. They were empty. "Laurel, this is amazing. I've never done so much in sales in one night. You've done a fantastic job."

Laurel blushed. "It wasn't me. You sold yourself with that super performance. People really enjoyed your act. Hey, I've got to go. Can you handle things from here?"

I nodded. "Most definitely. I'll take the bins back to the bus, and should be back in plenty of time to see you play."

Laurel left, and I cleaned the table off and stacked the empty bins onto the hand truck and wheeled it to the bus. We had everything locked up, so I used my keys to unlock the storage bin and stowed all the gear, relocked everything, and headed back to the stage. When I got to the wings, Toby's band looked ready to go. Gabe was twirling a drumstick, Fran had her bass strapped to her body, and Laurel was checking a couple of strings to make last-second adjustments.

I looked around, but didn't see the man himself. "Where's Toby?"

Fran rolled her eyes. "He's such a diva. Sometimes he waits until the last moment to join us, and sometimes he waits until we're already playing before he steps onto the stage. The man's a big drama queen."

Outside, the crowd was getting restless and was clapping in rhythm, as if the act would draw the band out.

"We can't wait anymore," Russell said as he turned his frown into a smile and headed on stage. The cheering intensified as he took to the microphone. "And now, here's what you came here tonight to see! Ladies and gentlemen, The Toby Madden Band!"

Russell rushed offstage and Gabe, Fran, and Laurel took his place. Gabe knocked out a beat on the drums, and Fran added a bass line a few seconds later. Laurel stood poised and ready to go. There was only one thing missing. I looked around behind me, but there was still no sign of Toby.

Russell growled. "Damn him." I saw him signal to Laurel, and Laurel started on her fiddle. Unlike most shows, the opening number was going to be an instrumental song without the headliner.

Russell turned to me and put his hand on my shoulder. "Could you do me a favor and go check the bus while I see if he's passed out in the men's room?"

"Sure thing." I left the building and half-walked, half-trotted to Toby's tour bus. I knocked on the door and called for him, but no one answered. Hurriedly, I knocked louder, and tried the handle. The door opened.

I climbed the stairs onto the bus. It had a similar layout to mine, but since it was a top-of-the-line model, and a good thirty years younger, it put my old bus to shame. I opened doors and checked rooms as I made my way from the front to the rear, and eventually I came to the last door. I rapped on it, then gently pushed it open. The moment I saw him, I knew he was going to miss his dramatic appearance onstage.

Toby Madden was dead.

CHAPTER FIVE

When I first saw Toby, he was lying on the bed, face down, one arm sprawled over the side, like he had thrown himself there after a hard day in the mines. My initial, more optimistic thought was that he had a few too many beers and had passed out as a result, but he remained too still, too quiet. I walked around the side of the bed, and when I spotted his eyes, they stared straight off into the great beyond. I rushed from the bus and ran back to the stage.

Russell was already back where I had left him, and I gulped for air, and bent at the waist with my hands on my hips as I reached his side. I wasn't a runner. "Call the police. Toby's gone."

"Gone? What do you mean, gone?"

I took a gulp of air and straightened my stance. "I mean he's…" I looked around to determine if anyone was in earshot. "Dead."

Russell opened his mouth, closed it, and repeated the process. He looked like a guppy tracking down food. "I don't understand."

I pointed in the general direction of the bus. "He's in his bed.

Dead. I saw him. You need to call the police."

Russell stood, unmoving. He picked a great time to play the statue game.

"Give me your phone," I ordered.

Russell complied, and I took it and called 9-1-1. After a few seconds, the operator answered the call, and I explained what had happened and where we were. I hung up and offered the phone to Russell, who was still doing his best fish impression.

"What are we going to do? People are expecting him to play," Russell said, as if that happened to be the most pressing thing on his mind at the moment.

I shook my head. "He's sung his last song."

I looked out at the stage. The band was on their third instrumental song, perhaps their fourth, and I could tell the crowd was growing restless at the lack of Toby's appearance.

"You've got to stop the show," I said.

Russell nodded and finally came back into his own head. "Yes. Of course, you're right. Thank you."

Russell stepped onto the stage and said a couple words to the band that I didn't catch and approached the microphone. "I'm sorry folks, but because of unforeseen circumstances, Toby Madden won't be able to play for you tonight. I appreciate you coming out, and please stay safe on your way home."

As expected, a chorus of boos erupted from the crowd, but when they watched Fran, Gabe, and Laurel leave the stage behind Russell, they disbursed.

We clustered in a small circle. Fran took off her bass guitar and handed it to a roadie. "What's going on?"

I waited for Russell to say something, but when I looked at him, he was already looking at me, expecting me to break the bad news.

I exhaled, followed by a deep breath. There was only one way to rip off this bandage. "Toby's dead. I found him on the bus."

Fran's eyes jumped immediately to mine. "You're kidding."

I stayed silent, but I held her gaze.

"You're not kidding," Fran realized.

Laurel started crying. Russell moved closer to her and put his arm around her shoulder, and she surprised me by taking a step farther away from him. "What happened?" Laurel asked.

"I have no clue. I found him and came back here and called the police."

If on cue, sirens whined nearby, got louder momentarily, then stopped.

"I'd better go. Since I found him, the police will want to talk to me," I said.

I left the stage and headed for the bus. I noticed there was already one squad parked beside it, and off in the distance, I spotted another two cars and an ambulance coming up the road. Much of the crowd that had left the amphitheater clustered around the immediate area.

I waited by the patrol car's hood for the trooper to appear. A couple of minutes later, he stepped off the bus and approached me.

"You the one who called this in?" I looked at the officer. I read the name Marvin printed on the name tag of his county-issued brown deputy's shirt.

"Yes. I'm Codi Cassidy. I found him. He was supposed to play tonight, and didn't appear for the show, so his manager asked me to search for him. No, Codi with an I, not a Y." It was a common mistake, and I thought I'd help him out as he took notes.

Another man was making a beeline for us. I could tell by the way he moved he was the person in charge.

"What do we have here?"

"Well, Sheriff, I just arrived. There's a DB on the bus. This is the person who called it in."

"Sheriff Cross, ma'am. Can you explain what happened here?"

I sighed. I hated repeating a story, but I did. When I finished, the sheriff nodded in understanding and addressed the deputy. "Lee, why don't you work with the others and clear the crowd, okay? Close the park if you need to."

Deputy Marvin took the order and left us. A paramedic stepped into the place the deputy had recently vacated.

"Well?" the sheriff asked.

The paramedic did a head-bob toward the bus. "He's gone, Sheriff. I can't tell for sure how long, but probably more than an hour. You'll need to get your investigative team on there before we can move him. It's too tight inside, and we'll have to carry him out without a gurney."

"Okay. I'll tell you when you can take him," Sheriff Cross said.

The paramedic returned to the ambulance to wait, and the sheriff moved to his car, opened the trunk, and returned with a duffel bag. He caught the questioning look in my eyes and took a moment to explain.

"It's a little joke around here. I am the investigative team."

While I waited, I walked back to my bus and retrieved my lawn chair from its storage cubby. After I set it up, I wanted to check on the kids. Fortunately, Merle, Dolly, Waylon, and Willie were all present and accounted for. Although I typically left their doors open so they could come and go as they pleased, I thought it best to keep them locked up for the time being. It was not the time and place for either a skunk or a three-legged raccoon, regardless of how cute and friendly they were.

I sat and waited. After ten minutes, Gabe appeared over the horizon, pulling my wagon behind him, and Laurel and Fran followed him, each with a guitar in hand. They stopped when they got to me.

"We brought your gear," Gabe said as he stopped right before me.

"Thanks. I appreciate that. Everything except the wagon

goes on the bus."

Gabe reached for the door. "The door's locked."

I stood and fished the keys from my pocket. "Sorry about that. I must have locked it when I came out last time." I unlocked and opened the door, grabbed my guitar case, and hauled it inside. The interior was dark, so I flipped on a few lights. I carried my guitar to my room and set it down next to the bed.

Gibson wasn't in his normal place, so I looked around for a moment until I finally spotted him curled in a ball underneath my table.

"Stay in here, okay? Only for a little while."

Gibson threw me a half-hearted meow in protest as I closed the door behind me. When I got to the common area, Gabe was there holding Bozeman's pedal assembly and Bozeman's two guitars were at his feet. Laurel was cradling my laptop, and Fran was looking in my fridge.

"Follow me with that," I said.

Gabe did as he was told, and I opened the gear storage door and directed him where to place the pedals. He headed back for the guitars and stored them in the room and returned to the parlor and slid into the booth next to Fran.

I pointed at the laptop that Laurel still held, cradled like a baby to her breast. "I'll take that."

Laurel looked down. "Oh, yeah. Okay."

She passed me the computer, and I set it on the kitchen counter next to the microwave.

"Might as well have a seat." I pointed at one of the two remaining chairs in the room. Laurel sat in one. I took the other.

Gabe looked from person to person until his eyes settled on me. "So now what?"

I shrugged my shoulders. "Beats me. Have any of you seen Bozeman?"

Laurel and Gabe shook their heads.

Fran sat forward. "Nope. Not since you played. Wonderful

set, by the way. I'd never heard any of your songs before. I really enjoyed it."

"Thanks." It wasn't the best of times for a compliment, but I took it anyway.

We waited in awkward silence for a good fifteen minutes for someone else to say something, but no one did. I felt relief washing over me when I caught a knock at the door.

"Come on in," I called.

A second later, Sheriff Cross appeared and stood tall before us. "I need to ask you all some questions. Would you mind coming with me? Let's start with you."

He pointed at Laurel, who sat closest to him. She got to her feet and followed him out of the bus.

"Interrogation time," Gabe said. He developed a sudden interest in his left thumbnail and started picking at it.

The wait continued. Perhaps an hour passed before Laurel returned, and Sheriff Cross removed Gabe from the room.

Laurel returned to her original chair and looked at the floor.

The silence was driving me nuts. "Well? What was that about?" I asked.

Laurel glanced at Fran, then looked at me. "I'm not supposed to talk about it until he's talked with everyone."

I nodded in understanding. It seemed logical to me. Once again, silence descended on us like a warm blanket as we waited.

The knock on the door returned, and the sheriff came for Fran. Laurel's brow furrowed as she noticed Gabe wasn't with him. "Where's Gabe?" Laurel asked.

She moved to get to her feet, and Sheriff Cross motioned for her to remain seated.

"Don't worry about him. He's outside. Sitting right outside the door here."

I stood and looked out the window. Sure enough, he was in my favorite lawn chair, the interest in his fingernail returned. I nodded at Laurel. "He's fine."

Laurel relaxed, and Fran followed the sheriff off the bus.

I wondered if I should turn on the television or make some tea or something when Laurel whispered in my direction. "Have you talked to them yet?"

"Just a little. Why?"

"Did he ask you about anyone you think could have done it?" Laurel asked.

"Done what?"

"Toby. The sheriff said someone murdered him."

That was news to me.

"He's been getting alibis from all of us and asking questions about everyone else. He wants to know if anyone saw anything," Laurel said, keeping her voice low.

"Go back. Someone murdered Toby? How?"

Laurel looked at the door, then back at me. She leaned so far forward in her chair I thought she'd fall over.

"They said they strangled him to death. How horrible."

I nodded in agreement and sat back. It was horrible.

"They also want to know—"

Laurel stopped the moment she detected the door open. A heartbeat later, Bozeman appeared.

I felt a sense of relief. "Hey, stranger. Where have you been?"

Laurel looked at Bozeman, then at me, then back at Bozeman. "I have to go. I'll talk to you later." Without another word, she scampered from the bus in a hurry.

An expression of confusion passed over Bozeman's face. "What was that about?"

I shrugged. "Don't know. So where were you?"

Bozeman took off his hat and placed it in the seat Laurel had just vacated. "After the gig, I talked to a few fans, then left for a walk around the park. What's going on? What's with the cops and the ambulance?"

"You don't know?"

Bozeman shook his head.

"Someone strangled Toby to death. I found him on his bus when he didn't show up for his set."

Bozeman's expression changed, and his face looked like he had just taken a big gulp of curdled milk. "Wait, what? Murdered? You're kidding."

"Come here." I got up and had Bozeman join me at the window. I opened the blinds and pointed outside to where the ambulance was still waiting. Several of the sheriff's department were milling about, trying to appear busy. "Does that look to you like I'm kidding?"

Bozeman slowly shook his head and took a seat at the table. "What's going on?"

"The sheriff's been taking statements from Toby's band mates, and I imagine he's going to want to speak to us too."

Bozeman was about to respond when the sheriff appeared. "Ms. Cassidy, could I have a few more words with you?" He passed an odd look in Bozeman's direction as I stood, then he escorted me from the bus.

When I stepped off the last stair, I noticed Gabe had moved the lawn chair to the end of the bus, and there were two deputies guarding my door.

"Right this way." I followed the sheriff away from the buses and over to a small picnic area. On a picnic table was an upside-down notepad covered by a rock. His duffel was on the ground next to the table. "Have a seat."

I sat down at the table and swung my legs in so I was facing forward. Since he was just under six feet and had a bit of a paunch, he put only one leg over the bench when he sat.

"How long have you known the deceased?" the sheriff asked.

"I just met him yesterday."

He picked up the rock and set it aside, turned the paper over, and jotted a note, then looked at me. "You just met? How did you become his opening act, having never met?"

"He's Bozeman's friend. They go way back," I explained.

"Where were you between the hours of six-thirty and eight?"

That was an easy enough question. "I was setting up our merch table, then we played our set."

"Do you have any witnesses?"

I smirked. "Of course. Everyone here did. We started promptly at seven and finished just a couple minutes past eight."

"No, I mean, can anyone verify you setting up your merch?"

"Yes. Laurel was with me the whole time. She and Fran ran it while I was playing."

"Where was Mr. James during that time? Didn't he help?"

"No. It only took the two of us. There wasn't a lot to do."

"Can you vouch for his whereabouts for the half hour before you took the stage?"

Could I? I thought hard about the question, and I realized there was really only one answer since I had interacted with only one person during that time frame.

Sheriff Cross didn't wait for an answer. He set the pen on top of the pad. "What about the fight Mr. James had with the deceased earlier today?"

My stomach did a somersault. I finally understood where this was going. I didn't lie, but I did try to soften things.

"It was just a disagreement."

"Over what?"

"One of Toby's songs. Bozeman recognized it as a song he'd written back when they were partners and wanted to ask Toby about it."

"Mr. James wasn't happy about it?"

I shook my head.

"Did he threaten any physical violence to the deceased?"

You mean other than to kill him? I thought. "He was upset, sure, and I don't blame him. But Bozeman's a big teddy bear, and he wouldn't really hurt anyone."

"Would you be able to explain this?"

Sheriff Cross leaned over and took a plastic evidence bag from the duffel. He had a crumpled piece of paper in the bag, and when he turned it around, I recognized it right away.

"It's sheet music. To the song we were supposed to join Toby on during the encore."

The sheriff nodded. "Right. Can you guess how this piece of paper got jammed into Toby's throat?"

That one I had no answer for, although I wanted to provide a sarcastic one. In the end, I found it best to keep my opinion to myself.

"Thank you, Ms. Cassidy. That's it for now."

As the sheriff took a couple more notes, I excused myself and stepped back to the bus. The deputies near the door eyed me warily, but neither prevented me from entering. Bozeman was sitting right where I left him.

"Bozeman. Be honest with me. Where were you after the rehearsal?"

"You know where I was. I went for a walk."

"Yeah, but where?"

"Just here. Around the park. This place is massive. There are a couple of ball diamonds over that way, a soccer field, a disc golf course, a kid's playground, and a bunch of nature trails. Why do you ask?"

"Did you talk to anyone? Interact with anyone? Anyone recognize you?"

I stared at him as he searched through his memories.

"No. I didn't talk to anyone. It was pretty quiet over there. I saw a couple of guys playing disc golf, but they were way off in the distance and probably didn't see me. Come on, Codi. What's up?"

"Bozeman, listen to me." I walked over to him and placed my hand on his upper arm. "Remember earlier today when you got into that fight with Toby?"

"Yeah. Of course."

"Remember the part where you called him a thief and said you should hang him?"

Bozeman blinked. Twice. Then realization struck and struck hard. His chin dropped to his chest, and he rubbed his forehead.

"The cops think I did it, don't they?"

I nodded. "I'm pretty sure you're suspect number one."

"And they asked you about the threat I made? And where I've been? You told them?"

"Bozeman, look at me."

Bozeman looked back up at me. I could see a mix of fear and sadness in his dark brown eyes. "Have you ever known me to tell a lie?"

He shook his head.

"Would you want me to?"

"No. Of course not. You're the most moral person I've ever met, Codi. I know it's not in you to lie to anyone. Even if you did…"

I knew where he was going. "Yep. Even if I did, there were a half-dozen others who heard what I heard and saw what I saw."

"I'm so screwed."

"Did you do it?"

A flash of anger shot through his eyes, followed by a moment of hurt that I'd even asked the question.

"No. I didn't. You know I could never."

I believed him. I'd seen him angry, and I'd seen him drunk, and I'd seen him say or do stupid things. But none of the things I'd witnessed in the past led me to believe that Jesse James was a killer.

I heard the door open, and someone climbed the steps. I looked over and saw Sheriff Cross and Deputy Marvin standing there. The sheriff had a pair of handcuffs in his right hand.

"Bozeman James, I'm Sheriff John Cross. What can you tell

me about the death of Toby Madden?"

Bozeman denied it right away. "No. Only that I didn't do it."

"Where you were this afternoon after the fight?"

Bozeman looked up at the sheriff, but didn't answer.

"Can you tell me anyone you interacted with, anyone to provide any kind of alibi?"

Bozeman stayed silent.

"Okay. We'll do this down at the station. Stand up and turn around."

Bozeman complied with the orders, and the sheriff placed Bozeman's right wrist in the cuffs.

"Bozeman James, you're under arrest. What was that?"

"I said my given name is Jesse. Bozeman's my stage name. That stays here."

Sheriff Cross chuckled. "No kidding? Jesse James? For real?"

Bozeman nodded. "Codi, give him my driver's license, okay?"

"It's in his room. Can I go get it?"

The sheriff nodded. "Marvin, go with her."

The deputy followed me into Bozeman's room, and I found Bozeman's wallet on his table right where he left it most of the time. I grabbed the wallet, removed his license from the plastic window, and returned the wallet to the table. The license I handed to the deputy, and we returned to the main room. The deputy passed the card to the sheriff, who examined it carefully. Cross put the license in his left shirt pocket, and from the right, he extracted what looked like a laminated business card.

"Son of a gun. Okay, then. Jesse James, you're under arrest for the murder of Toby Madden. You have the right to remain silent."

Bozeman struggled against his cuffs. "Wait, no. You've got the wrong guy! I didn't do it! I'm innocent!"

"Bozeman!" I got the attention of all three men in the room, and they each turned to look in my direction. "Shut up. Use that right."

Bozeman nodded, and the sheriff went back to the recital. "You have the right to remain silent. Anything you say can and will be used against you in a court of law. You have the right to an attorney. If you cannot afford an attorney, one will be provided for you. Deputy, escort him to my car, please."

Deputy Marvin took Bozeman's elbow and guided him to the bus door, and then they were both gone.

"What happens next?" I asked.

The sheriff looked at me. "Well, I'll hold him at the county jail until he can get a preliminary hearing in front of a judge. We're a little backed up, so it'll probably be Tuesday or Wednesday next week at the earliest."

"What do you think the judge will do?"

"It really depends on the judge, but since this is a murder charge, I suspect the judge will hold him over for trial. I shouldn't say anything about anything, but I'd recommend you get him an excellent lawyer, and line up a bail bondsman. Otherwise, he'll stay with us until he goes to trial."

I followed the sheriff down the stairs and into the night. At some point, they must have removed the body because the ambulance was gone, and there were only three police cars left at the scene. In the car nearest me, I saw Bozeman in the back seat, head down, not moving. Sheriff Cross got into that car and drove off.

At Toby's bus, I saw Deputy Marvin bark orders to another deputy who was busy sealing the bus door off with police tape. Once the task was done, Marvin nodded and drove off in his own car. The final deputy, whose name I did not know, slipped behind the wheel of his own vehicle, but didn't go anywhere. I suspected his order was to stay on site and protect the crime scene from the public, even though they'd cleared the public from the park.

Up into the dark California sky I looked, just in time to see a shooting star pass overhead, and I took a moment to make a wish. I hoped had the strength to carry it through.

CHAPTER SIX

I was sitting in a captain's chair, cuddling with Gibson, when I heard a soft knock at the door. I wasn't expecting company, nor did I want any, so I ignored the sound. A few seconds later, the knock resurfaced, this time a little louder. I ignored it again, but the knock returned for a third time, and this time it sounded like whoever was pounding on the door was using a baseball bat to do so. I relented.

"Come in," I yelled.

The door opened with a squeaking noise I hadn't noticed before, and I made a mental note to write that down in the log I kept for Bozeman's bus maintenance tasks. The thought of Bozeman and the running list of chores I had for him around the bus made me sad and I wept again, which sucked because I hate to cry.

"Hey, hey there. Are you okay?" It was Laurel. She dropped the backpack she was holding, kneeled down, and wrapped her arms around me, which sucked, because I hate being held while I cry. If I have to cry, I like to do it alone. It seemed to make Laurel feel better, though, so I didn't pull away. So, I wept for a bit and threw in an intermittent sob for effect. I took a deep breath, and Laurel loosened her grip and pulled away.

She got back to her feet, headed into the kitchen, and returned with a paper towel, which I used to blot my eyes.

"I'm sorry," I said.

"Hey, there's no need to apologize to me. This has to be hard on you."

Laurel noticed Gibson. "Oh, I hope I didn't squeeze your skunk. I didn't notice him before."

I shook my head. "No. He's not a skunk. It's Gibson. He is my cat."

When he heard his name, Gibson picked his head up, which he had nuzzled into my torso, and looked around. He saw Laurel and reached out a paw.

"He likes you. Shake his hand."

Laurel did as she was told. "Nice to meet you, Gibson."

Gibson responded by struggling to his feet. He did a move I called the Halloween Kitty in which he stretched out, arched his back, and pointed his tail straight up in the air. He held the pose for a five second count, jumped to the floor and lazily walked to his food bowl.

I sniffled one last time, wiped my eyes, and blew my nose. I balled up the paper towel and tucked it under my leg.

"What are you doing here?"

"I've got a favor to ask. Would it be okay if I stayed with you? Only for tonight?" Laurel pleaded.

"Don't you want to sleep on your bus? It has to be far and away more comfortable than mine."

"We can't. The police taped it off and we can't return to it until they finish their investigation. They let us on under supervision long enough to grab enough personal items for a couple of days, but that's it. We can't get back on until they release it."

I got up and threw the used paper towel in the kitchen trash.

"Just you?"

Laurel nodded. "Gabe's roughing it in the park. He's got a tent and a sleeping bag. Russell and Fran rode into town to find a hotel."

I thought about it for a moment. I didn't remember the last time I'd spent time alone on the bus. It had to have been months. I didn't mind being alone, and it's not like it scared me or anything, but it was always nice to have another person around if I wanted to talk. I could always talk to Gibson, Merle, and Dolly, but they never held up their end of the conversation. I was going to decline, but then my heart dropped when I saw Laurel standing there looking put out like Little Orphan Annie.

"Okay. You can stay for one night. You'll have to sleep out here, though."

She nodded. "Deal. That chair looks comfortable enough."

"No, not the chair, silly. The dinette there will convert to a bed. Here, I'll show you."

Laurel got out of the way, and I moved through the steps for her. First, I removed the tabletop, then the tables support pole from the middle. I removed a bench cushion and set the table into the built-in tracks, which bridged it across the space. Then I rearranged a couple of pillows to make the mattress, and with a little effort and sixty seconds worth of time, Laurel had a place to sleep.

Laurel looked at it like it was a magic trick. "That was easy. I guessed it converted, but I didn't know how."

"I'm sure you would have figured it out with some trial and error," I said.

Laurel picked up her backpack and put it on the bed and sat in the other captain's chair.

"Why didn't you go to town for a hotel?" I asked.

Laurel's cheeks reddened. Apparently, I'd touched on a sensitive subject. "I'm… a little short on funds. I haven't gotten paid in a while, and what little I make, I send home."

"How long is a while?" It wasn't my business, but my curiosity got the best of me.

Laurel thought about it. "I don't know. Two months, perhaps three."

That surprised me. "That long? I was expecting you to say a week or two at most. Why so long?"

Laurel shook her head. "You'd have to ask Russell that question. He and Toby never discussed the finances with us, and anytime Gabe, Fran, or I needed spending cash, we'd just ask Toby, and he'd reach into his pocket and hand us money."

"So, you're saying there was money? It wasn't a case of just being broke?"

"Oh, no. There was plenty of money. Toby always had a roll of bills in his pocket, like in those old gangster movies. He and Russell never lacked for anything, and there was always food and drink on the bus, and we never ran out of gas, so there must be cash coming from somewhere."

"Did Fran or Gabe get paid regularly?"

"I never asked. Since most of our needs are taken care of, it wasn't a big deal if we got paid sporadically."

I understood the logic to a point. I found when on the road, there wasn't a lot of time to go on shopping sprees, and as long as we didn't need food or other necessities, there wasn't much need for money. Most of it got deposited into the business account.

"You don't have a bank account to draw from?"

Laurel looked offended at the question, and I wanted to apologize for digging in too deep, but she answered before I said anything.

"Of course I do. I earmarked most of that for my grandmother. She's been ill, and I have a care provider for her."

"I'm sorry. Where is she?"

"Bakersfield," Laurel answered.

"You see her much?"

"When I can. I'm sure you recognize how it is with the schedules we keep."

I nodded. The life of a traveling musician wasn't all people romanticized it to be, especially when it came to staying in contact with family and friends.

"Although, I do video chat with her every day. Hey, Codi, if it means anything coming from me, I don't think Bozeman killed Toby. He doesn't seem like the type."

"Thanks. And he's not. Actually, it's a rare occurrence when he even loses his temper like he did today. The only other time I've seen that has been when he's protected me. All I need to do is clear his name. Sounds easy enough, right?"

Laurel nodded that she agreed, but the look on her face told me she didn't seem totally convinced.

"Do you mind if I ask you a few questions?" I asked.

Laurel brought her feet up below her and sat cross-legged in the chair. I had to give her points for that, since there was no way I could ever accomplish that acrobatic task. "Go ahead."

"How long did you work for Toby?"

Laurel gazed up at the ceiling for a while as she accessed her memory. "It's been more than a year. Fourteen, fifteen months maybe? They brought in me as a session player for his last album, and he asked me to stay as a regular in the band for this latest one."

"Did you ever have any trouble with him?"

"Like what? Like, did he come on to me, or did we fight, or whatever?"

I nodded. "Sure. Either, or both. Or more."

Laurel laughed. "A big no, and no. He and I had no animosity outside of the studio, and I wasn't really his type, so I never had to worry about him making a pass at me."

"What's his type?"

"Oh, the typical things that men go for. Tall, blond hair, blue eyes, thin, tan."

I smiled. "It sounds like you're describing Fran to a T."

"Almost. Frannie has hazel-green eyes, not blue, and she wears colored contact lenses, but still."

"Did they have a thing? Toby and Fran? Like, romantically?"

Laurel shrugged. "I don't know for sure. If they did, they kept it pretty well hidden. Ask Fran about that. I'm sure she'd be happy to tell you. She doesn't have much of a filter."

"How long has she been around?"

"Let's see," Laurel glanced back up at the ceiling. "Eight months? She wasn't around for the recording. She came in after Rusty left."

"Who's Rusty?"

"The old bass player. He'd been with Toby for years, then one day, he said he'd had enough, packed up his gear, and left us at the next city we came to."

"Sounds like they had a pretty big fight."

"They got into it something good all right, but I never figured out what they were fighting over."

I wondered if it had something to do with stolen lyrics. At least I had a lead on a suspect other than Bozeman. I got up, headed to the kitchen for a couple of cans of Diet Dr. Pepper and handed one to Laurel. She smiled, and we opened our cans and drank in unison.

"Have you seen Rusty around lately?" I asked, resuming my line of questioning.

"Sure did. I saw him last Saturday."

I raised an eyebrow.

Laurel reached into her pocket and extracted her phone. She clicked a few buttons, then passed the phone over to me. I looked at it and watched a video of a band playing at a theater. I watched half the song, then passed the phone back.

"Let me guess, the bass player is Rusty?"

Laurel took the phone and nodded.

"You know where and when that video was from?"

Laurel looked at her phone again. "A week ago Friday, Atkins Theater in Syracuse, New York."

Even I didn't think it was plausible that a guy would span the entire country to commit a murder.

"Rusty moved on and found a new band."

"He sure did. He's playing for someone now who's up and coming. The new guy has promise and will probably be bigger than Toby would ever hope to be."

I let out a heavy sigh. "Well, there goes my suspect pool."

Laurel smirked at me. "Don't give up so easily. You still got the rest of us. Me, Gabe, Fran, Russell…"

"Hey, that's true. Did you kill Toby?"

Laurel laughed. "No. I didn't kill Toby."

I wanted to take her at her word, but there were just a couple more things. "Did you ever leave the merch table during my set? Go to the bathroom? Get something to eat or drink?"

Laurel shook her head. "Nope. Stayed there from the time you left me until you returned."

"What about Fran?"

"Frannie's heart isn't really in sales. She showed up maybe ten minutes after you left, took a quick break in there to go do whatever she did, and left about five minutes before you came back."

"You know where she was?"

"Before and after, no. During, I'm pretty sure she wanted a snack because I saw her walk off toward the food trucks. Well? Did I do it?"

I looked at her in the eyes. "No. You didn't. No opportunity, no motive."

"I may be lying, you know. I might have shut down the merch table and did the deed and returned later. You wouldn't have noticed."

"No, you didn't. I checked the timestamps on the credit card transactions. At most, there was a four-minute gap between them. You didn't do it."

"I'm glad you believe me," Laurel said. She smiled at me, then took a drink.

"Me too. Hey, what about Gabe? What was their relationship like?"

Laurel stretched her arms in the air, then scratched her head. "Gabe's been with us for only a couple of months. He used to be in a metal band, then got shipped off here for some strange reason. To be honest, I don't understand it. He's a good drummer, but he's not a country music drummer, you know what I mean?"

I nodded. I understood. Different music, different rhythms, and methods.

"Gabe and Toby ever have any words?"

"No, but I imagined there would have been some, eventually. Toby was always on Gabe about his playing. Gabe was doing the best he could to learn the music, but occasionally, he'd make little slip-ups. Not enough to affect the song ever, but it was enough to throw us other musicians off."

"His playing presented a problem with the band?"

Laurel paused again. "I'd say not really. Fran's not the best bassist in the band, but she always keeps the correct tempo, and I have to give her credit for that. I mean, she's got a head for timing. She could play something in a four-four-time signature and have a different person around her playing in three-four, and she'd still hold her own. Anyway, Gabe always leaned on that. Every time he messed up, he just followed Fran right back to where he should be."

"But Toby didn't like that, I'll bet."

"No. He sure didn't. I remember one time at rehearsal, the kid kept messing up and Toby kept getting angrier and angrier at him. I mean, it was frustrating. We had to restart the same song at least eight times by then, and I was sure Toby wanted to bust his guitar over Gabe's head by then."

"What happened?"

"In the end, Toby screamed a bunch of things at Gabe I don't want to repeat, then he left and returned to the bus."

"And what about Russell? Does he have any issues with Toby?"

Laurel frowned. "Ask Russell that one. To be perfectly honest, when we first met, Russell was a little too forward toward me, if you know what I mean. Since then, I've been trying my best to keep my distance and never be alone with him if I can help it."

I nodded. "Smart girl."

Laurel yawned, and I felt bad for her. It had been a long, emotionally taxing day, and I realized how tired I was, too.

"I'll get you some bedding."

"Great. You have a place I could change?"

"Sure. Use my bedroom. It's at the end of the hall."

Laurel picked up her backpack and hauled it into my bedroom and closed the door. While she was gone, I retrieved a set of sheets, a blanket, and a pillow from the equipment room and made up the bed for her. I heard the door open. When I looked over, Laurel stood before me wearing flannel pajama bottoms with penguins on them, and a T-shirt that featured an alien flashing the peace sign. I couldn't help but grin.

"I like the ensemble."

Laurel plodded to the bed while I checked that all the blinds were properly closed, then I locked the door. "If you need anything, I'm right down the hall. And if anyone comes to the door, don't answer it. Come and wake me up, okay?"

Laurel nodded and pulled the covers up to her chin. "Good night."

"Good night, Laurel."

I shut off the lights and walked through the dark to my bedroom. Within a few minutes, I got changed and dove into my bed. I felt Gibson jump on the bed, and within a couple minutes, he was lying on my chest and purring. I didn't know if I'd be able to sleep, but there's something calming about a cat's purr and within scant seconds I drifted off to dream land.

The next morning when I got up, Gibson was no longer with me, which was unusual for him. After I slid into some jeans and a shirt, and used the bathroom, I went to check on my guest. I found her back in the captain's chair, reading a book. Gibson was on her lap, licking his tail.

"Good morning," I said, trying to sound chipper.

Laurel looked up and smiled. "Good morning. Sleep well?"

"Surprisingly, yes. You didn't need to do that."

Laurel had folded up all the bedding and turned the bed back into a dinette.

"It was no trouble. I appreciate you letting me stay over. What do you plan on doing today?"

I opened the fridge and looked in. There was plenty of food for the kids, not so much for me unless I wanted a salad for breakfast. "Well, after I get cleaned up and feed the animals, I'll probably venture into town and see if I can visit Bozeman."

"Want some company?"

I thought that over, then agreed. "Sure. But you have to have breakfast with me, too. Does that work for you?"

Laurel nodded and put down her book. "Sure, if I can grab a shower first."

"Let me feed the beasties, and I'll come with you. I could use one myself."

Laurel slipped into more appropriate clothes while I dropped off a plate of vegetables for Merle and Dolly. Both were sleeping and didn't notice me. Willie and Waylon were both chittering away when I opened their cage. I could tell they were happy to get into the morning sun when they jumped to the ground and bounded away without so much as a hello. I cleaned out their abode and dropped a couple of shelled walnuts into their dish as a surprise treat upon their return. When I turned around, Laurel was there, backpack in hand.

I went back aboard the bus and grabbed my shower things, and met her back outside. We didn't talk as we walked to the shower house, but I thought it was still nice to have someone along with me. Like the previous day, the place was empty. We each selected a stall, showered, dressed, and headed back.

We were halfway to the bus when we saw Gabe headed in the opposite direction. Based on his look, he had gone through a rough night. His hair looked tussled, and I thought his face seemed paler than the day before. Something else I hadn't picked up on was that he wore eyeliner. I only noticed it then because it had smudged overnight, giving him a wicked raccoon appearance.

"Good morning, Gabe," Laurel said to him as I wondered if she was always so perky in the morning.

"Hey." Gabe's greeting came out more like a grunt than an actual word.

I thought this would be an excellent time to get his take on things. "While I have you here, you mind if I ask you a couple of questions?"

Gabe thought otherwise. Without stopping, he grunted again and kept walking.

Laurel turned her smile on me. "He's not really a morning person."

After we returned to the bus, I made sure I had my phone, wallet, and keys on me. I was never much of a purse-girl, especially since I usually had my guitar case with me that I could shove stuff in. Laurel was already outside waiting for me, and I locked up the bus and was ready to go.

"I wonder how far we need to walk to get to the jail."

"Oh, we have three options on that. We could either walk, which is about four miles from here, or, if we wanted to wait for Neil, he could give us a ride, or we can get a rideshare."

"Who is Neil?"

Laurel turned and pointed toward the police car stationed near Toby's bus. "Deputy Neil over there. His relief doesn't get here for another hour, but he said he'd give us a ride if we needed it."

Before I could answer, my stomach rumbled loud enough for Laurel to hear.

"I'll get us a rideshare," Laurel said before I could answer her question. "Can you share the cost? I scraped up about thirty bucks, but that'll have to last me until I can get to a bank."

I agreed. Laurel performed some magic on her phone, and within fifteen minutes we were in the back of a van headed toward town. The driver dropped us off at a diner. We entered, and I happily worked my way through a Denver omelet with toast while Laurel downed a plate of pancakes. As she ate, Laurel used her phone to find the county jail, which, to our mutual joy, was only four blocks away.

After breakfast, we walked to the jail. Out front there was a marble monument dedicated to law enforcement surrounded by benches. Laurel got comfortable on a bench and pulled a book from her backpack as I entered the building.

I didn't know quite how to frame my question as I approached the desk. What was Bozeman? Inmate? Suspect? I wasn't sure as I made my request. "I'd like to see someone in your custody, please."

The desk sergeant looked at me, then tapped the small sign next to the desk that read 'no visitors without prior approval'.

"I'm here about his lawyer."

The sergeant looked me up and down. I was wearing blue jeans, a T-shirt, a zippered sweatshirt, and a baseball cap to hide my blue hair.

"You don't look like no lawyer to me," he said.

"No. I'm not his lawyer, I'm his business partner. I'm here to see who he wanted to contact for his lawyer. We have several that we use." That was a little white lie, since we had only one.

But in my defense, my person knew people.

I could tell the sergeant was about to deny my request when Sheriff Cross appeared. "Ms. Cassidy. Sign in there and come with me."

I looked down and jotted my name on the visitor log, along with who I was going to see. The desk sergeant collected my hat, phone, keys, and wallet, and handed me a visitor's pass to clip to my shirt. From there, I followed the sheriff into a small room, and he directed me to a chair. He left, and I waited. Ten minutes later, the door opened, and Bozeman entered, followed by a deputy, and then the sheriff.

Sheriff Cross nodded, and the deputy left the room. "You can take all the time you need, but since you're not legal counsel, we'll be watching and listening."

He pointed to the ceiling corner to show us the camera. He unlocked Bozeman's left handcuff, ran it beneath a metal bar attached to the table, and cuffed his wrist.

I waited to speak until he left the room, which was silly, considering we were being recorded. "Are you okay?"

"Yeah."

"You don't look so good. Didn't you sleep much?"

"Not really. The only benefit to being a murder suspect is I didn't have to share a cell with anyone. They think I'm a menace to society."

"Who should I call? You got a lawyer in mind?" I asked.

Bozeman shook his head. "Never needed one. I certainly don't want a public defender, though. Think Mac could find me one?"

Morris MacDonald was our entertainment lawyer. He stepped in when we had things that involved complicated contracts. Like when we hired musicians, producers, and booked studio time when we cut new records. Occasionally, we had him look over the paperwork when we got approached by a larger music festival or some other promotion company. He was a good guy, and always weeded out the bad deals for us.

"Criminal law is outside his area of expertise, but I can get a recommendation from him."

Bozeman nodded. "I've been trying to wrack my brain around who would do this, but I can't come up with anyone. And since they've got the witnesses saying I made the threats, they're pretty sure I'm the guy. I wish we'd never found that notebook."

"What do you mean?" I asked.

"Well, I wasn't one hundred percent sure he'd stolen my song until I confirmed it with the book. I mean, I thought it sounded familiar when we played it at rehearsal, but that happens all the time since so many songs like to sample from other songs."

"Wait, Bozeman. That notebook would prove you wrote the song."

"Yeah, so?"

"I mean, if you could prove you wrote the song, wouldn't it make more sense to sue the pants off him and the record company for copyright infringement?"

Bozeman exhaled. "Again. Yeah, so?"

I smiled at him. "So that takes away your motive. You'd be better off keeping him alive. You wouldn't see a penny with him dead. I need to find that notebook."

CHAPTER SEVEN

Laurel and I caught a rideshare back to the park, and she followed me into my bus. I had Laurel take a seat at the dinette while I headed to Bozeman's bedroom to search for the notebook. The room appeared just as I'd left it when I got his license, except his wallet wasn't in the same place I'd gotten it from. Bozeman was, in a word, a neat freak. Although he'd never been in the Army, you wouldn't guess that by looking at his room. He made his bed with military precision, and he stowed everything away where things should be. The only place that usually looked cluttered, and I'm using the word cluttered loosely here, is his table. The surface usually held his wallet, phone, and other things he used most often. Currently, there was a notebook, along with a mug filled with pens and pencils. The notebook was open to a page which was half-filled with lyrics and chords. No doubt a new song he was working on. I turned the notebook over, and sure enough, it had a blue cover, not a red one.

I did a quick spot check around the room, including under the bed and in the small closet, but saw no signs of the book I wanted.

"He must have put the thing away," I said to myself, and that made sense because he had an annoying habit of putting things back when he finished with them. Half the time I don't think he even realized he did it. It was automatic.

After I left his room, I trekked to the storage room and retrieved Bozeman's banker's boxes. I remembered him pulling out only two, but I found four, and I wrestled them all out into the hall and set them next to the dinette table. I opened the cover of one and set the box on the table.

"Here, help me sort through this. We're looking for a notebook with a red cover."

Laurel and I dug through the box and repeated the exercise Bozeman and I had gone through the previous day. Although this time, I didn't have his organized mind to ease the task.

When we finished, we had four books stacked on the table.

I took the top one and gave it to Laurel and grabbed the second for myself. "Let's go through these first."

"What are we looking for?" she asked.

"That song Toby wanted to put out as his first single. The one he planned for us to sing together at the encore before the big fight happened. Somewhere in one of these books are the handwritten lyrics that Bozeman wrote years ago, and they seemed to be a perfect match to the sheet music Russell gave us. Sheet music."

Where did I put the sheet music? I assumed what the sheriff had in the evidence bag was Bozeman's copy, but where did I put mine?

Unlike Bozeman, who will put things away when he's not using them, I will often leave items out a little longer before I deal with them, much to Bozeman's chagrin. Sometimes it gets to where he will stow them somewhere without telling me, and I'll spin in circles, sometimes literally, trying to find the item I wanted.

My go-to place was the dinette table, but since Laurel and I currently sat at it, I knew that was out. I checked the kitchen counters and the kitchen trash before I returned to my bedroom to search there. Unlike Bozeman's barracks, my room looked a little more lived in. Today, I pulled the bedcovers up and stacked the pillows on the bed. I did that more for Gibson's benefit than mine since he liked to sleep on the top of the pile. I checked my table, which currently held my computer, a bunch of random, unrelated papers, a handful of guitar picks, and an inkless pen that I'd yet to throw away. No sheet music.

I exited my room and walked back to Laurel. "You wouldn't have a copy on you, would you?"

Laurel shook her head. "I left my copy on the other bus. Are you sure you had yours?"

"I'm pretty sure. I had it when I followed Bozeman back here. Then we rifled through the notebooks, and I'm pretty certain we compared them to his copy, because he crushed his into a ball, and I had folded mine. Then he left, and I gave the kids a snack, and…"

I remembered where I put the thing, so I stepped to the fridge, opened the door, and right on the top shelf I discovered the piece of paper, neatly folded in half. I brought the paper back to the table, opened the sheet, and set it sideways so we could both use it for reference. Of course, I tried to act as if keeping things in the fridge was normal for everyone.

"Page through the book and find the sheet that matches the lyrics. I'm pretty sure Bozeman had a different title, but I don't remember what he called the original."

"I understand," Laurel said as she reached for the book.

Laurel and I started working through our respective books, and the bus stayed quiet. Until Laurel suppressed a laugh, then didn't hold it back.

"What's so funny?" I asked.

"I did the same thing once; except I lost my phone. Usually, I set my alarm for seven, but for some insane reason, I woke up early, and I was the only one up, and I must've put my phone in the fridge when I looked for something. Of course, at seven, the alarm rang, and wouldn't turn off, so it kept dinging. You couldn't hear it from outside the fridge. When Russell opened the door, he suspected someone planted a bomb in there, so he slammed the door shut and ran off the bus."

"That's not funny." Then I pictured Russell scampering away and I laughed. "Okay, that's a little funny."

I completed my notebook first, then grabbed another. I was about halfway through when Laurel closed hers and reached for the last book. When I finished, I waited for her. Nothing. I put all four notebooks back in the box and returned the box to the storage room while Laurel started on the next box. In the second box, we had five notebooks to search through. In the third box, there were zero red-covered ones, and in the fourth box we found six. After two hours, we'd been through all the boxes, and the notebook wasn't in any of them.

"Now what?" Laurel asked. She had a good question.

"Hold on a minute. Bozeman took the notebook with him back to the stage when he confronted Toby. Did you see that?" I asked.

Laurel nodded. "Didn't miss that. He almost shoved it up Toby's nose."

"Then the ruckus started. Maybe Bozeman dropped the book and didn't pick it back up before I dragged him away. Do you remember seeing it?"

Laurel thought for a moment. "No, since I focused on the fight. I suppose it might still be by the stage."

"I doubt it. There must have been, what, three or four dozen people backstage after that? Someone probably found it."

"Let's go check, anyway," Laurel said.

I imagined that would be a hopeless exercise, but Laurel was right. We should at least look and cover that base. Together, we walked to the amphitheater and stepped backstage. It was empty. Russell's road crew had packed up all the gear and equipment and hauled it away. From what I could tell, the crew was top-notch, and they impressed me with the pack out. Not even a remnant of gaffer tape remained on the floor where they'd affixed the cables.

"Someone might have picked it up and put it in a random road case," Laurel said.

I exhaled. "Yeah, you're probably right. Someone found it and shoved it in with a random piece of gear. Now all I'd have to do is find that gear. Is the sound and lighting company the same as what you guys normally use for a show?"

"I don't think so. This was supposed to be a big deal, so the record company brought it all in from Los Angeles."

I frowned. If that were true, there would be no way I would track that stuff down. It would either be in a warehouse or on its way to the next gig.

"Damn," I said.

Laurel took me by the arm. "Come on, there's nothing here. Let's go back."

I let Laurel lead me from the stage and we trudged back to the parking lot. As we got closer, I noticed two things. The first was more police activity on Toby's bus. The second was Gabe sitting nearby, still in my favorite chair. We walked over, and he grunted in acknowledgment.

Laurel pointed at the police. "What's going on?"

Gabe shrugged. "I'm not sure. Perhaps the cops are doing another pass-through for evidence or whatnot. The one guy yesterday said they were going to do that."

We watched for a while. I saw Sheriff Cross appear once again, front and center, with his duffel bag in tow.

"We didn't have time to talk this morning. Can we do it now?" I asked.

Gabe shrugged again. "I guess."

"I take it you're not much of a morning person?"

"No. Not really. You know how it is in this life, right? Sleep until mid-afternoon, get up, do a gig, party all night."

I didn't know what life he was talking about. It certainly didn't fit with my experience of show business, which rarely included after-parties or staying up all night. Unless it meant driving to the next show. Bozeman and I usually woke up early every day, or at least I did, since he did all the driving and sometimes slept in after a long road trip. There was too much on the business side of show business to do.

"How did you get along with Toby?"

Another shrug. At least his shoulders were getting a good workout. "Okay, I guess."

"I heard he would come down on you during rehearsal," I stated, more like a fact than a question.

He paused. "Where'd you hear that from?"

"It doesn't matter. Is it true?"

"Sometimes. But he was like that with everyone, not just me."

I didn't respond and waited for him to fill in the growing uncomfortable silence. It worked.

"Okay. I admit, it's taking me a bit to get in the groove. I'm used to different music. When I was with the other band, I could play anyway I wanted, and I got to do solos."

"And Toby?"

"Oh, he was always on me. Gave me music to listen to and expected me to learn how to drum from that. Anytime I missed a beat, it seemed he wanted to beat me. But look at it from my perspective. I'm new to this. I don't know about all this country stuff, and I made a mistake coming here."

"Anyone else have any trouble with Toby?"

Gabe erupted out of the chair so fast there could have been a spring beneath him. Laurel took an instinctive step back, but I stayed anchored in my spot.

"Why are you bothering me? Ask her. Ask any of them. I

don't care. Just leave me alone!"

He huffed with a side of growl, and he puffed his chest out. A scowl crossed his face, and I knew at that moment that I misjudged the kid. I thought he was a shy wallflower type trying to find his way. But with the outburst, he seemed to be one of those internal-volcanic types who was prone to blow under the least provocation.

He stepped closer. The toe of his shoe contacted mine. I didn't back away, though.

"Before you say anything else, or do anything you'll regret later, I suggest you look to your right," I said.

He hesitated a moment, then looked. Deputy Marvin was leaning up against his car, watching the whole thing.

Gabe took a step to the side. "I have to use the bathroom. Don't talk to me again."

Gabe turned and stomped off toward the restrooms. I took advantage of his leaving and folded up my lawn chair, carried it back to my bus, and locked it in the storage space where it belonged.

"Is he always like that?" I asked.

Laurel looked back, probably to confirm he hadn't returned. "Not always, but he's been getting worse over the last couple of weeks. I wonder what his issue is."

"Well, if I had to guess, I'd say he has two issues. Anger and drugs."

"No. Do you think?"

"I think he's using something. What, I'm not sure. He probably ran out of whatever he was on a couple of weeks ago, and now he's going through withdrawal and can't handle it," I said.

"Are you sure?" Laurel asked.

"Not a hundred percent, but somewhere in the high nineties. I've seen it before. You think Toby or Russell are wise to his problem?"

It was Laurel's turn to shrug. "I have no idea. Obviously, it's a surprise to me."

I was about to comment on something else, but before I could, Sheriff Cross approached.

"Ms. Preston, do you know where Mr. Davidson is?"

Laurel answered right away. "Well, if he's not here, he's probably still in town. Why do you need him?"

"We're all done here. We've got a few things we're taking for evidence. Here's a list of the things we took." The sheriff handed her a sheet of paper that she didn't bother looking at. "Also, I'm releasing the bus, so you're all free to go back. You two have a nice day now."

We watched as the sheriff casually moved to his truck, got in, and drove off, leaving Laurel and me there alone.

Laurel glanced at the paper, seemed disinterested, then looked at the bus. "I hope they didn't lock up behind them. I don't have a key."

"You don't have a key to your own bus?"

"No. Russell was always paranoid about security. Only him, Toby, and the driver had a key. It usually wasn't an issue, since one or more of them were always around."

"Driver? I don't think I met a driver."

"Yeah. I'm not surprised. He and Toby didn't get along much. Steve's only around when we need to drive somewhere. When we're not on the road, I don't see him much."

"That seems odd to me. What was their riff?"

"No clue. You'd have to ask Steve. I imagine he'll be around today sometime since we're free to leave. Speaking of which, I'd better call Russell."

Laurel took her phone from her pocket, looked at it, and returned it. "My phone is dead. Like an idiot, I forgot to grab my charger yesterday. Come on, let's go get it."

I followed Laurel, and luckily for us, the sheriff had left the door wide open.

"Whoa. I hope I don't have to clean up this mess."

I looked around the common area, and I could tell the sheriff and his crew had done a thorough search. Although they destroyed nothing, they'd also returned nothing to the exact spot it had been. There were seat and couch cushions awry, items spread out, and I could see in the kitchen area where cabinets and drawers were half or fully open. It looked like a small tornado had come through since I'd been on the bus last.

"I'm going to check out Toby's room," I said.

Laurel nodded and took the lead, but turned left into her space while I headed to the rear. The door was open, and I stepped into the room and saw pretty much what I expected to. The bedding was gone, and there was black fingerprint dust everywhere. There was a bedside table with a drawer, so I reached over and slid it open. Inside the drawer was an open pack of AA batteries. I also found a crossword puzzle book, a broken pencil, and an adult magazine with the photo of a blond with very impressive breasts on the cover. I closed the drawer and turned my attention to the closets. It didn't take me long to determine there was nothing to see.

I left Toby's room and returned to Laurel's. She didn't have a room as much as she had a dedicated sleeping space. She didn't have a door, but a sliding privacy partition. Her space included a cot-sized bed with under-bed storage, and a small nightstand that also served as a table. She also had a small portable wardrobe that appeared to be made of cheap press board.

She saw me hovering and screeched at me. "Don't come in here!"

"Why not?" I asked.

"It's embarrassing," Laurel said.

"It's not so bad." I stepped over and sat down on her bed. I couldn't confirm, but I think her mattress had concrete instead of padding. "Before I bought my bus, Bozeman and I were touring the country in an old van from the seventies. We spent more time broken down on the side of the road than we did playing music."

Laurel relaxed and checked her phone. It was on the charger, but apparently didn't have enough juice just yet.

"Really? You and Bozeman slept in a van together?"

"Sure did. It had a bench seat that fit me perfectly, but poor Bozeman had to sleep either sitting in the passenger seat or curled around the gear in the back. Most nights, he slept in a pup tent outside, which wasn't so bad in the summer. Or so he claims. You'll have to ask him about it sometime."

"What do you suppose this is?" Laurel asked.

I looked at the finger Laurel was holding out to me.

"It's fingerprint powder. They probably wanted to get the prints of everyone who was on the bus. Did they take your prints when they questioned you yesterday?"

Laurel shook her head as she grabbed a tissue and wiped the powder away. She used the same tissue to clean up the mess on the nightstand.

"They might, just to exclude you as a suspect," I said.

"You sure know a lot about police work for a singer."

I smiled. "Well, my dad was a cop."

I let it go with that. I didn't mention that dad was actually a detective in the Denver Police Department, nor did I talk about my proclivity for getting in and out of mysteries.

"You mind if I look around the bus some more?"

Laurel wrinkled her nose. "I don't know about that. Toby had a pretty strict rule about not going into each other's spaces, you know?"

"I get it. Everyone needs their privacy, right? You think I could at least use the toilet?"

"That you can do. Go back toward Toby's room. It's on the right."

I left Laurel to her cleaning and stepped into the hallway. I waited for a moment to ensure we were alone, since I didn't want to get caught by anyone. Then I drifted in the general direction of the bathroom. After I looked back to see if Laurel was watching, I opened one door and saw a small bunk area. I assumed it was Gabe's, based on the messy appearance and drumsticks laying on the bed.

The next room over belonged to Fran, I assumed because of the bass guitar leaning in the corner, and the pictures of herself hanging on the far wall. She must have done modeling work at one point, because none of the shots appeared to be selfies or from a point-and-shoot camera. Her room was a little larger than Gabe's area, and although the bed was small, the area was extensive enough for a real closet and a dressing table. She'd cluttered up the dressing table with bars and bottles of makeup and other cosmetics that I never used.

Russell's room was next, and it was larger than Fran's, and smaller than Toby's. His amenities included a full-sized bed, a closet, a bookshelf stuffed with books and papers, and a small desk. Although I wanted to enter that space and rummage through all his papers, I didn't want to break my promise to Laurel. I just took in what I could see from the doorway.

I saw nothing of use to me, so I left his room and went to the bathroom. Their bathroom was larger than the one on my bus and included a full-sized toilet, vanity, and a shower stall that looked like an old phone booth. I did my business, washed my hands, and went back to Laurel.

"Everything good in here?" I asked.

I found her still scrubbing away at the nightstand. "No. I don't think this powder will ever come off. Can you look around to see if they messed anything else up like this?"

Someone had folded over the covers on her bed, as if they had gone through the three under-bed drawers, and one wasn't closed properly. I crouched down, opened the first drawer, and peered in. It was where Laurel kept her personal hygiene and beauty supplies. The second drawer she'd stuffed with socks and underwear. The third one, which wasn't on its track, was full of music books and correspondence. As I fixed the drawer, I thumbed through the contents.

"That's all music and old letters and cards from friends and family. I trained in classical music before I switched over to country, so I like to practice that stuff sometimes to keep sharp."

I pushed the drawer closed and sat back on the bed. "Hey, Laurel, I'm sorry. I didn't mean to pry."

Laurel looked into my eyes for a second. "Yes, you did."

I thought she was serious for a moment, but then she laughed. "Got you. It's okay. I've got nothing to hide. Check the closet, will you?"

I opened the wardrobe and looked inside. It had three sections. The top half had a bar to hold hanging clothes. From what I could tell, Laurel's wardrobe consisted mostly of jeans and casual shirts. There was also a rain jacket, a heavy jacket, and two sweatshirts on hangers.

On the left side were three drawers. I opened and closed all the drawers quickly. Two held T-shirts, and the third held four pairs of shoes, three casual, and one pair of black high heels that matched the only dress she had hanging in the closet.

On the right side, below the hanging clothes, was an area to hold just about anything, and in that space, there were four violin cases. I touched one, and a violin bow tipped over and fell out of the closet.

Laurel heard the sound and glanced over. "What's that doing out? I keep all the bows in their cases when I'm not playing. It's too easy to damage them otherwise. Find out where that goes and put it away, will you?"

I took out the first case and looked in. Not being a violinist, I didn't really know what I was looking at, but it looked like the type of violin I'd seen in every orchestra I'd ever watched. The top had a place for bows, and this case held two of them. I closed the case and opened the next one. This violin looked like it was from outer space. It was missing most of its body, although it had the neck, fingerboard, and chin rest the previous one had. It looked to be missing the body.

"What is this?" I asked.

"Oh, that's my new baby. Full electric. I love it and want to transition over to it. Not as temperamental onstage as a classic violin."

"You weren't playing it yesterday, were you?"

"No. Toby won't let me play it in concerts. It didn't match the pure country image he wanted."

The violin had its bow, so I moved on to the last case. I put the case on the bed and opened it.

"Laurel? How did this get here?"

Laurel looked over and she and I stared at the red notebook stuffed into her violin case.

CHAPTER EIGHT

Laurel looked flustered and spoke up immediately. "I didn't put that there."

I reached into the case, removed the notebook, and opened the cover. Sure enough, Bozeman had written his name, along with the date range the contents spanned. I had a choice to make: whether to believe Laurel, or throw her back into my suspect pool. If I had the supplies, I would dust the thing for fingerprints myself. Regardless of the training my dad gave me, I never picked up that skill and always smudged them, thus making them unusable.

"You don't know how this got here?" I asked.

"No. Of course not!"

"This isn't the fiddle you played last night?"

"No. That's an old one I never use. Check this out. I damaged one of the tuning pegs, and I haven't gotten it fixed yet. About two months ago, I broke it."

I picked up the violin and glanced at the instrument.

Even though I didn't play a violin, I knew enough about stringed instruments to tell one of the tuning pegs seemed askew. I placed the violin back in the case, added the bow, and closed it.

"Besides, how would I know the notebook would be so important? And if I took the thing, why would I hide it where someone would find it so easily? It's not like I have a lot of secret stashes here. I don't even have a locking door. Anyone who wants can come in here." Laurel waved her arms around the small space and then crossed them in defiance.

I thought Laurel made a lot of really excellent points, even though she sounded a little defensive. Although I imagine I'd be acting the same had our positions been reversed.

I looked at Laurel. Nothing about her body language suggested she tried to hide anything from me, and I did believe deep in my heart that she knew nothing about the book.

"What's going on here?" a voice said.

Laurel and I ended our staring contest, and both looked over to see Gabe standing in the hall.

Laurel picked up her phone and held it out. "I forgot my charger. I need to call Russell and tell him we got the bus back. Or do you want to?"

Gabe huffed. "Yeah, right. Like I'm going to call him. Have fun."

He left, and I guess based on his direction, he was going to his own room.

"You mind if we go back to your bus? I don't want to be with him here alone."

I thought she made a reasonable request, so I followed Laurel off her bus, and she followed me onto mine. Truth be told, it seemed empty without Bozeman around, so I was happy to have her there.

"Looks like someone's hungry." Laurel pointed at the floor.

I looked over and noticed Gibson's stainless-steel bowl was empty, and he was sitting before it, hitting it repeatedly with his paw. It made a slight ting sound every time one of his nails came into contact with it.

"He can be demanding when he's hungry. Here, take this and find the song."

I gave the book to Laurel, and she sat down at the dinette while I opened a cabinet and pulled out a plastic container filled with dry cat food. "Are you hungry, little man?"

I filled the bowl about a quarter full, then set it back on the floor. Gibson rubbed against my leg, then moved in for the snack while I put the container away.

"Laurel, would you like something to drink?" I asked.

"Yes. I'll take a bottle of water if you have one."

I nodded and opened the fridge. There was plenty of Bozeman's favorite beer in there, but no water. I walked back to the storage room, found the fresh case I remembered we had in there, pulled out a couple of bottles, and sat down opposite Laurel. I slid the bottle to her, and she opened it up and drank half before setting it down.

"Thanks. I was really thirsty," she explained.

I thought it was odd when Laurel got to the last page, then closed the book and handed it to me.

"It's not in there. Wrong notebook."

I made my signature confused scrunchy face. "It has to be. It was the only notebook that he removed from the bus. The rest are all in storage."

Laurel passed me the notebook, and I opened it and started from the beginning. I wanted to rush through, but I took my time so I wouldn't miss it. I remembered it was somewhere in the middle, but I didn't find it, and soon, I too got to the end without success.

"This makes no sense." I lifted the book and shook it in the air. "It has to be in here."

As I shook the book, a piece of paper about the size of a single snippet of confetti floated down and hit the table. Laurel and I both followed its fall, like we were watching a bald eagle descending on a field mouse.

"Oh, no," I said.

I started from the beginning and paged through the notebook again. This time I paid particular attention to the margins on the spiral end where the paper connected to the wire. I found the spot I was searching for and pulled out another snippet of paper.

"Someone ripped it out."

Laurel leaned in and examined the book. "How can you tell?"

I lined up the two pieces of paper on the table before her.

"When they ripped out the pages, they left behind a couple bits of evidence."

"How do you know Bozeman didn't rip those pages out himself? It might be he didn't like whatever he was working on and removed it. It could still be the wrong book."

I flipped back a few pages, didn't find what I wanted, then flipped forward a few, and pushed the notebook back to Laurel. "If he didn't like something, he put an X through it and moved on."

Laurel looked at the page and the ink marked that stretched from corner to corner. She paged through the book and discovered another one shortly thereafter.

"I'd also be willing to bet that if I counted the pages in the other notebooks, they would match the count on the cover," I said. "And this one would be short, although I don't want to go through that experiment. Unless you'd like to."

"No. I'll take your word for it. What does it mean?"

"It means someone understood the importance of that notebook and that song, and I mean to figure out who it was. Got enough battery to call Russell yet?"

Laurel checked her phone, nodded, and made the call.

*

Two hours later, Laurel and I were sitting outside, me in my favorite chair, Laurel in Bozeman's, when a car pulled up and Russell and Fran emerged from the vehicle. Russell carried a backpack and a computer bag. Fran had a carry-on suitcase, and she looked like she was returning from the airport.

Fran waved her fingers at us before she climbed onto the bus, but Russell didn't acknowledge us at all.

Fifteen minutes later, Fran stepped off the bus carrying a large mesh beach bag. She had a pair of flip-flops wedged in the side, the top of a bottle of shampoo sticking up from a pocket, and there was a towel under her arm.

"Hey, keep your eye on things here for me, would you?" she said in our direction.

Without waiting for Laurel to answer, I jumped out of my seat and double-timed my gait until I almost caught up with Fran. Since she was taller than I was, I had to walk a little faster than I normally would just to keep up with her.

"Fran. Hey, Fran, slow down!"

Fran stopped, looked behind her, noticed it was me, and smiled.

"Hi, Codi."

"Do you mind if I talk to you?"

"Sure. Walk with me. I'm sorry about your friend getting arrested. He seemed like a nice guy. I was hoping to spend some time with him."

On instinct, I rolled my eyes. It seemed Bozeman had a knack for attracting attention in practically every place we played. Not that it surprised me since tall, dark, and handsome didn't go out of style, and he always kept his six-pack, regardless of how many twelve-packs he put away. To his credit, though, he rarely caught any of the passes that women threw his way. When he did, he never brought a date back to the bus, which is something I was eternally grateful for.

"Well, I hope you get your chance. I called a lawyer this morning, and she thinks we can bond him out by tomorrow."

Fran smiled. "How nice for him."

"I'm sorry about Toby. How long were you with him?" I asked.

Fran smiled again. "You mean with his band, or with him personally?"

I stopped in my tracks. "Are you saying you had a relationship with him?"

"It wasn't really a relationship. I had certain needs, he had certain needs, and we fulfilled them for each other."

"What did you need?"

"A job. When I was a young girl, I wanted to be a model or a guitar player. I modeled, but I assumed that wouldn't last forever. I mean, I'm going to turn thirty in a couple of years, can you imagine? And take a glance at this…"

Fran pointed to her forehead. I expected to view a pimple or mole or something, but her skin looked fine to me, even without makeup.

"At what?"

"Look. Closer. A wrinkle. Can you imagine?"

I couldn't. I probably had a few myself, but I never scrutinized myself in the mirror to seek them out.

"Lucky for me, my parents had me take up guitar when

I was a little girl, and when I became a teenager, I switched over to bass guitar. Bass is sexy."

I nodded, wondering where this was going.

"I was lucky enough to be a part of a photo shoot for some of Toby's promotional material, and I told him I wanted to be a part of a band. He had me audition, and before I even finished, I was in the band. How fortunate for me."

I didn't want to know, but I had to ask. "Okay, so what did Toby get out of the deal?"

"Sex. What else?" Fran said it so matter of fact that the candor surprised me.

"Isn't he married?"

"Yes. Well, he was, I guess. Millie, or Maddie, or something from Texas or Virginia. I don't recall. I only met her a few times," Fran said.

"Did she learn you were having an affair with her husband?" I asked.

Fran shrugged. "It beats me. I don't really care. He got lonely on the road, and she refused to travel with him, so it was her own fault."

I didn't understand the logic behind that, and at the moment, it didn't matter. In my mind I added Millie, or Maddie, or something to my suspect list, but I doubted in this case the wife did it. I didn't think she would understand the significance of the stolen song. Still, I wanted to ask about her.

"Did you ever have any minor or major disagreements with Toby?"

"Oh, no. None. Not one."

"I heard he could be hard on people during rehearsals."

"Who told you that? Gabe?" Fran asked.

I didn't confirm or deny.

"If it was him, then yes, he was tough on that little pill-popper because he plays the drums like one of those wind-up monkey toys. But Toby said nothing negative to me. Ever. Well, that's not true. He did once, but I corrected him, and he fell into line, and I never had a problem with him again."

"How did you correct him?" I almost didn't want to get the answer.

"Why, Codi, I denied him access to these."

Fran dropped her bag and lifted her shirt, exposing her bare breasts to me. I have to say, based on that move, she was self-confident. And perky. She dropped her shirt while I looked around to check if anyone else had seen her, but we were alone.

"Did Russell ever have any issues with Toby?" I asked after a pregnant pause.

"Oh, sure. They argued all the time about everything. Anything else? I really need a shower."

"No. I guess not. Thanks for speaking to me."

Fran bent over to retrieve her bag, and I took a step toward the bus, then stopped. "One more question. Do you get paid regularly?"

"Sure. Every week like clockwork. Every other week direct deposit from the record company, and on the off weeks I get a cash bonus from Toby." Fran winked at me, then frowned. "I guess I'll need to find a new band."

Fran shrugged and walked away. I figured she didn't kill Toby. No motive, and without him, she'd lost her position and her perks. After I exhaled, I headed for the bus.

I was about halfway back when I felt someone's eyes on me. I looked to my left, saw no one, turned to my right, and spotted Tommy Skye leaning up against a tree. He waved, but when I took a step toward him, he turned around and ran across the field.

I was in no mood to chase him, so I didn't. Instead, I continued on and took my seat next to Laurel.

"Did you know Toby and Fran were sleeping together?" I asked.

"It wouldn't surprise me if Fran was sleeping with everyone on that bus. Well, except me, she's not really my type. Let me guess, did she show you her boobs?"

I nodded. "How did you know that?"

"For some nutty reason, she gets off on being topless. It drove Toby nuts, and I can't imagine what it did for Gabe."

"She mentioned in passing, Gabe is a pill-popper. You ever catch him taking anything? Notice any bottles lying around?"

Laurel shook her head. "Not that I can remember. Although pills are a little more discrete than say, something like cocaine, right? I mean, he could hide them in an aspirin or vitamin bottle, and no one would be the wiser."

I agreed. "Look, I hate to ask, but is there a way you could look around? See if he is hiding anything like that? Don't feel pressured, though. You can say no if you want to, and I won't think anything less of you, and won't say another word about it."

Laurel didn't answer right away, and I could tell she was mulling it over, which only added to the respect I had growing for her.

"If it'll help your friend, I'll do it," she said after a few minutes.

I nodded, and we sat together in silence for a few minutes. Then, without a word, Laurel rose and left me.

"I saw you talking to that nasty woman."

To my credit, I didn't flinch when I caught the voice, but I looked to see where it came from. It was Tommy, who had positioned himself behind my bus so I could only see his head.

"So what?" I asked.

"Did she tell you lies about me?"

"Why don't you come over here and we'll talk about it."

"No. I don't want them to see me. Come over here," he said.

"Okay, but I'm warning you, I'm armed."

"Fine. I'm not."

I picked up my chair and hauled it over to where Tommy was. Rather than set it down hidden from anyone else's view, I placed it at the end of the bus's bumper, just in case. "What's up, Tommy?"

"Did she tell you lies about me?"

I got up and adjusted my chair. I had placed one leg on top of a hole, so I was in danger of tipping over at any point. "No. She never mentioned you."

Tommy rolled his eyes, then spun in a full circle. "Sure. She didn't tell you she got me kicked out of the band?"

Before he spoke those words, I was ready to remove myself from the conversation, but now he had my rapt attention.

"How did she do that?" I asked.

"Let's just say it had something to do with those melons she showed you. I'd been with Toby since the beginning, before he even cut his first record. You look at the liner notes, and you'll see me in there. Tommy Skye on bass. Played with him through the dirty bars and county fairs. Then that album hit, and he started becoming a celebrity. When the second album dropped, that's when we started doing the bigger tours. Auditoriums. Arenas. Inside gigs, you get what I mean?"

I did. Some people didn't mind playing outside, and I've enjoyed a cool breeze running across the stage while under the fiery lights. But the benefit of the indoor concert was the show continued on as scheduled. Didn't have to worry about rain, snow, lightning, heavy winds, or excessive heat. Or insects, or birds. I even had a bat swoop over my head once.

"So, what happened?" I asked.

"We were doing a promotional piece for an upcoming tour, and someone thought it would be a good idea to bring a couple models in as arm candy for Toby. We'd done it before, but the only difference is, this model plays bass and never left when the shoot was over. Before you would say lickity split, I was off the tour and hitchhiking my way back home."

"Where is home?"

"I'm originally from Kansas, but I've been in L.A. for about twenty years now."

"Were you mad at Toby?"

"Of course. But oddly, I couldn't blame him. He's always been a sucker for a big-boobed blond."

"Is his wife a big-boobed blond?" I asked.

"Allison? No way. She's an average-looking brunette. She's the type where if you passed her on the street, you wouldn't even glance at her."

"So then, why did he marry her?"

"I think they were high school sweethearts."

"Any chance she lives around here?"

Tommy gave me a Cheshire Cat grin. "And found about her husband's indiscretions and did him in for revenge? Nope. Sorry. She lives somewhere in upstate New York with her parents."

"Oh. Did you ever do any songwriting with Toby?"

"No, sorry, ma'am. I'm strictly a player. Never had much of a talent for writing. Tried it once, but it didn't work out for me. I'm sure you get it."

"Sure. It's not for everybody. Do you know who he collaborated with?"

"Not really. I wasn't a part of that. I didn't get involved

until there was a song to play. Sometimes I helped on the music end, suggesting riffs, or runs, or key, but that was about it."

"Hmm. Did you ever observe anyone accuse Toby of using their songs without permission?"

Tommy gave me the grin again. The first time, it was odd, this time, it was bordering on creepy. "You'll like this one. We were at a concert at some venue in Tennessee doing a soundcheck. Out of the blue, we got interrupted by a guy who came right up to the stage and started screaming at Tommy about stealing his song. Had a lawyer there with him and everything."

"What happened? Did the guy get physical?" I asked.

"No. Just a lot of shouting went on. The venue security came to throw the guy out, but the lawyer stepped in and stopped them. Next thing in an odd turn of events, Toby and Russell are talking to the pair all nice and civil like. The lawyer took a sheet of paper out of his pocket and handed it over to Toby. He read it, gave it to Russell. Russell read it, then must have said something to Toby, because he took the paper back, signed it, and gave it back to the lawyer."

As Tommy spoke, I visualized the events in my head. "Sounds to me like Toby got caught and got a choice to settle on the spot, or get dragged into court, and since I've heard nothing about it, he must have settled."

"Yeah. If he had any money. We weren't exactly living high on the hog back then, especially with Russell managing things," Tommy said.

I sat back and folded one leg over the other to get comfortable. "Tell me more."

Tommy leaned up against the bus. He was pretty close to the chipmunk nest. I hoped Willie and Waylon were out somewhere playing a nearby tree and not wanting to get into their house for the next few minutes.

"Well, Toby always thought that Russell was taking more of the pie than just his normal cut. He told me about a time he went to ask Russell about the budget, then Russell kicked him out of the room and made Toby come back an hour later. Russell showed him the books, but Toby figured what Russell showed him wasn't the complete picture."

"Skimming a bit off the top, you mean? Fudging receipts and numbers and whatnot?"

Tommy nodded. "Yep. You got the picture good."

"So why didn't Toby fire him? Or get the record company to replace him?"

Tommy shrugged. "Soon after that, Fran was in and I was out. By that point, I didn't care who managed the band."

"Did you overhear the name of the guy who accused Toby of pilfering his work? Ever seen him before?"

Tommy shook his head. "No. But like I said, we were in Tennessee. Could have been anyone. You get how Nashville is. There are so many songwriters there, you could use them to pave the way to Hawaii. Then have enough left over to create a different route back."

I had to laugh. I had heard that line before, although I didn't remember where. It reminded me of that old saying about every server in Los Angeles having a screenplay ready in their back pocket in case they served lunch to a big-name producer.

"Did you see the argument yesterday? Between Bozeman and Toby?" I asked.

"Yep. Saw the whole thing. It reminded me of the other time I just told you about. Except Bozeman didn't have a lawyer with him."

"Do you think Bozeman killed Toby?"

Tommy took off his baseball cap and scratched his head.

A few strands of hair came away when he did, and he looked at them indifferently and let the breeze take them before putting his hat back on.

"No. I don't. I've known Bozeman a long, long time, and I don't expect he has the stomach for it. The cops have the wrong man. I'm certain of it."

"You seem to know all the players, so tell me, Tommy, who do you think did it?"

"Well, if I were a betting man, I'd put my money on —"

Tommy was ready to spill the proverbial beans, but then I heard a yell from behind us.

I turned in my chair and saw Russell rushing toward us. He was screaming something, but I couldn't make out the words. "What do you suppose he wants?"

I turned back to Tommy, but Tommy had disappeared like a shadow at midnight. "Tommy?"

I looked back, and Russell was still on his way. He was wearing a light green polo shirt with his jeans, which was a mistake since the sweat from his exertion was darkening the fabric. It wasn't a good look. I wanted to give Willie and Waylon some space, so I picked up my chair and moved it back to where I normally had it near the bus door. I sat down just as Russell arrived.

"Hey Russell. What's up?"

CHAPTER NINE

"What was he doing here?" Russell demanded.

"Oh, not much. Just talking to me."

Russell eyed me with suspicion. I wondered if he was the paranoid type who always worried about what was being said about him. Since recent conversations didn't paint him in the greatest of lights, I didn't blame him for it.

"You wanted to talk to me, so talk," he said.

He got that right. I wanted to talk to him, and the more people I spoke to, the more questions I had for him. What should I accuse him of first? Fund theft? Copyright infringement? Murder? Toby's infidelity? So many choices, so little time. I threw him a softball.

"It's a shame about Toby. I really liked him. Were you two friends long?"

Russell looked at me with some apprehension. "We've known each other for a fairly long time, yeah."

"It's quite the rag-tag band he has, isn't it? I mean, if you put Toby, Fran, Laurel, and Gabe together in a room filled with musicians and told everyone to divide into a group, I wouldn't see it forming naturally."

"I don't get what you're saying."

"Well, take Bozeman and me, for example. When we met, I looked for someone to play the lead guitar. I had somewhat of a vision of what I wanted. So, I asked around, got a few names, did a few interviews, listened to people play. That's when I found Bozeman, and we had this natural chemistry that makes our partnership work. I don't feel the chemistry in Toby's band."

"Good thing you're not in the band, then. I've got things to do. Catch you later."

Russell pivoted to leave and got a step away before I threw out the next pitch. "Is it true Toby paid off a songwriter in Tennessee?"

That got his attention. Russell returned to my side. "You have no clue about that."

I didn't, really, since I had information based on a secondhand account. "Are you saying you didn't have to compensate a Nashville songwriter over a song Toby claimed to write? He figured out the theft, like Bozeman did, brought in a lawyer, and signed over the rights in a fair exchange for a payout. And I'll bet there was a nice non-disclosure contract to go with that as well. Am I right?"

Russell didn't speak. He simply stared at my forehead.

"Am I in the ballpark?"

Still no response, so I changed my approach.

"Fran seems like an odd addition to the group. Tommy out, Fran in? Can you tell me about that?"

"Nothing to tell. Tommy got erratic. He's a druggie. Everyone on the team knows we don't allow drugs anywhere near Toby."

"How do you find out Tommy did drugs?"

Russell sneered. "How would I not? He started having erratic behavior, losing weight, missing rehearsals. He had to be replaced. For the good of the band."

"And the best you found in all of country music was a bass player who happened to be a model at the time?"

"It's not like that. Frannie can play. She's a natural, and she's serious about her craft. She's well-respected. Ask anyone."

"Okay. How do you explain Gabe as the drummer? I understand he can't hold a beat."

Russell leaned in and pointed a finger at my face. "Come on, lady, I've had enough of you and your questions. I get what you're trying to do, trying to find someone else to pin Toby's death on, but the simple truth is, they've already got the right guy in custody. Your man."

Russell turned and stomped off. I didn't know what to do next, but then I felt a light tapping on my shoe. I looked down and spotted Merle nuzzling my leg. "Hey, Merle. Come here, buddy." I leaned over, picked him up, and set him in my lap. "What are you doing up already? Couldn't sleep?" In response, Merle shoved his nose up under my arm. I laughed.

"Stop, that tickles." I adjusted Merle so that I had access to his underside and gave his belly a good scratching. You would think a skunk wouldn't like that, but it was one of Merle's favorite things in the world.

"Well, where do we go from here? I'm not any further along with getting Bozeman out of trouble than I was yesterday. Do you have any ideas?"

In response, Merle spread out his legs and started smacking his lips, a sure sign he enjoyed his time with me. Merle must have realized I needed some attention because after fifteen minutes, I felt better and had a bit more clarity in my mind. I had devised a new plan, and the first step involved talking to Bozeman's lawyer.

"Come on, Merle." I picked him up and carried him with me onto the bus. I placed him on the floor, retrieved my phone, and found the number I needed. It took a few moments to dial the number, and the person picked up after the second ring.

"Jennifer Collins."

"Hi Jennifer. Codi Cassidy here. Bozeman James' friend?"

"Hi Codi. What can I do for you?" I imagined Jennifer leaning back in an oversized leather chair and putting her feet up on her desk. I also thought that happened the same way when all white-collar professionals talked on the phone.

"Do you have any word on Bozeman's arraignment?" I asked.

The line fell silent, and I thought she hung up on me, but then I heard a door close and some papers shuffle. "No, sorry. It may take a couple more days. From what I'm told, the county judge is out sick and they're trying to find a replacement for him."

"Is there any hope at all of getting him out soon?"

"No, sorry. Not until he's been before the judge."

"Is there anything you can tell me about Toby's death?" I asked.

"Sorry, I'm not supposed to say anything that would jeopardize the case. I'm sure you can understand that."

I hated not getting straight answers, but that only added to my persistence. "Hey, Jennifer, I'm trying to poke around here to see if I can find any answers, and I'm pretty much running out of options, so if there's anything at all you can tell me, please do."

Again, there was a long pause, and once more I thought she'd disconnected the call, but a second later, she whispered to me. "Okay. I would get in trouble with the court by releasing this, but I have a colleague at the morgue. The official cause of death is asphyxiation."

"Thanks. Anything else?"

"Yes. They did a rapid drug screening, and it turns out Toby had drugs in his system, although I won't have the full workup until the lab tests come back. They sent those to an external lab, so it will be a few days before I get the report. Hopefully, that will help you."

"Thanks. I appreciate the information," I said.

"I have to go. There's another client I have to meet with."

This time, Jennifer disconnected, and I put down the phone. I heard some crunching, so I did a quick glance over at Gibson's food bowl.

"Hey, Merle. I've told you a billion times that you shouldn't be eating the cat food."

I picked up the bowl and placed it on the counter. "You want a snack?" I opened the fridge and found the container of cherry tomatoes, which was Merle's absolute favorite. I counted only three remaining in there. Based on the space in the rest of the fridge, I guessed I needed to make a grocery run soon.

Bending over, I gave Merle a tomato, and he chirped like a bird as he grabbed it and munched on it. I was about to feed him a second one when there came a knock at the door.

"Codi? It's me."

"Come on in, Laurel."

Laurel entered, and once she was inside, she pulled a plastic baggie from her pocket and placed it on the counter next to the tomatoes. The bag contained a variety of pills and capsules.

"Sorry it took so long. I had to wait until everyone else was off the bus. This is a sample of everything I found in Gabe's room."

I picked up the baggie and looked at the contents. There were perhaps eighteen pills and capsules in all. A few things I recognized right away, including an aspirin tablet and a vitamin C supplement, but there were a few I didn't recognize. A squeal interrupted my investigation. I looked down and saw Merle looking up at me with a displeased look on his face. If a skunk did such a thing.

"Do me a favor and give Merle those tomatoes. One at a time, though, or he'll make a big mess with them. I'll be right back."

I retreated to my room, retrieved my laptop, and returned

to the dinette. Once I was there, I fired up my machine, and while I waited for that, I removed all the drugs from the baggie and lined them up on the table.

"What are you doing?" Laurel asked as she joined me. She still had one tomato in her hand, but I imagined that would be gone once Merle realized she had run away with his treat.

"Looking up these drugs." I handed her a white tablet. "See the imprint number on there?"

Laurel studied the pill. "Yeah."

"Each drug is supposed to have a marking like that. It helps to identify it. What is the number?"

Laurel told me, and I searched for it. "It's generic aspirin, just like I thought. What's another?"

Laurel picked up a capsule and read me the number from the side.

"That's an antihistamine."

We repeated the exercise until we identified all the over-the-counter drugs. There were three left. One was a capsule with a green body and a cap the same color as a robin's egg. The other two were pills. One was bright yellow with a sun stamped into it, and the other was a light purple adorned with what looked like the eye of Horus. Despite my best effort, I didn't identify those.

"What do you think these are?" I asked.

Laurel shook her head. "I have no clue."

"Where did you find them?"

"They were inside of a fake book. I wouldn't have found them; except I accidentally knocked the book over when I was reaching for something else. I have an idea. Take one, and I'll observe what happens to you."

At first, I thought she was serious, but then Laurel let loose the laugh she tried to suppress. "I'm sorry. I couldn't help myself."

The three unidentified drugs I put back in the baggie, and

the rest I swept into my hand and tossed them into the trash.

"Oh, Merle." I grabbed a paper towel and wiped up the remains of a tomato from the floor, then wet another towel and washed over the area again to clean up the sticky mess. I tossed the paper towels into the trash and looked around for Merle. He wasn't anywhere in the area, so I assumed he was somewhere searching for trouble.

The storage room, Bozeman's room, and the bathroom doors were all closed, which left my room as the remaining place to check. I looked in. Gibson was in his normal spot on the pillow pile, and although he lifted his head to look at me, he didn't move at all. I checked the floor under the table and in the closet, but I didn't find the skunk. I glanced at Gibson again and was going to ask him where his brother was when I noticed his mass was twice the size it normally was. It took me a step closer and a second longer to register what I saw. Rather than go back to his normal spot, Merle had curled up with Gibson for his nap.

I was lucky that all of my animals, most of the time, got along with each other. Although Gibson looked moderately annoyed by the disturbance, he wasn't angry about it. As far as Gibson was concerned, Merle was just some strange breed of cat who wanted to share a nap space.

"Everything okay?" Laurel asked when I returned to the living area and plopped into a captain's chair.

"Yeah. I'm just getting frustrated. You and I are certain Bozeman didn't murder Toby. I also recognize all the evidence points in his direction. I don't know where to go from here."

"Who's your money on?" she asked.

"A better question is who it isn't. I'm ninety-eight percent sure that you didn't do it."

A mock-angry look crossed Laurel's face. "Only ninety-eight percent? There's still a two percent chance you think I did it?"

"Yeah, but that's only because I don't want to rule anyone

out completely. Don't take offense. Deep down in my heart, you're innocent."

Laurel smiled. "That's good enough for me. I'll take it. So then, if not me, then who?"

"Fran? She had an affair with Toby."

Laurel considered it for a moment, then dismissed her. "No. I don't think so."

"Why not? Because she's a woman?" I asked.

"Of course not. Women commit murder all the time. I don't think she would do it because she doesn't really hide anything. She got her job because she slept with the boss. Everybody knows, and she doesn't care. She's sleeping with a married man. Again, she doesn't hide it, because she doesn't care."

"She'd care if Toby's wife suddenly showed up," I said.

Laurel chuckled. "That's a fact. Still, I don't see Fran caring about that, either. I doubt she'd get in one of those classic girl fights over Toby. She'd be more likely just to cut him loose and move on. She's like a shark in a tight skirt."

I nodded and agreed. It was a good analysis, and aligned with what my impression of her was too. Fran was the type to use her sex appeal to get whatever she needed. At least, until those wrinkles she worried so much about ended all that.

"What about Gabe?" Laurel asked.

"To tell you the truth, I had Gabe all but scratched off my list as well, but now that you found those drugs, I'm not sure. What you don't know is that Toby had drugs in his system when he died."

The look on Laurel's face told me it surprised her to hear that news. "Are you sure?"

"Pretty sure. I can't reveal my source, but I'll tell you that fact came right from the county coroner."

"Might there be a scenario where Gabe was supplying Toby those drugs, and something moved sideways and Gabe killed Toby?" Laurel asked. I liked the way her mind worked.

I shrugged. "Perhaps. Or it was the other way around. Toby was the dealer, and Gabe was the junkie? Then something moved sideways and Gabe killed Toby."

"That would explain why Toby always had a roll of money. Either way, Gabe kills Toby."

"Yeah. I'd have to push that one around in my head for a bit. What you haven't learned is that Toby was also giving Fran a bi-weekly cash bonus," I said.

That fact Laurel never expected, and it hit her hard. "No, really? Are you saying that I've been going without a paycheck and begging for pocket cash while Fran's been getting double?"

"It looks that way, yes," I said.

"What about Gabe? Has he been getting extra, too?"

"That I need to figure out yet."

Laurel shifted in her seat. I could tell the whole money thing bothered her, and I couldn't blame her for that. It seemed everyone was getting a cut of the pie while she had to go without. In the back of my mind, I wondered if she really knew all about that and extracted her cash along with a pound of flesh. It seemed plausible, so my confidence she hadn't murdered Toby dipped down to ninety percent.

"That gets us to Russell. What do you think about him?" Laurel asked.

"To be honest, there's so much there, he's almost too obvious of a suspect. Every time I talk to someone new, I get more details about potential shady stuff he's involved in. It seems to me, though, that Toby and Russell were equally complicit in their partnership."

Laurel shifted in her seat, then rose from the dinette, stood, and stretched her arms toward the ceiling. "Yeah, but again, could something have gone on there? Toby was going to turn on Russell? Wanted to cut him out of a deal? Or maybe Toby wanted to come clean and confronted Russell about it."

"Again, maybe, but either way, with Toby's career taking

off, why would Russell kill the golden goose if he was taking a percentage of the profits? That's the part that doesn't stick with me."

I was about to say something else, but as I opened my mouth, something hit the side of the bus. The impact wasn't strong enough to move the sturdy vehicle, so neither Laurel nor I were affected, but it surprised us both.

"What was that?" Laurel asked.

"Beats me," I said.

Since Laurel was already standing, she was almost out the door before I even got out of my chair. By the time I stepped into the afternoon sun, Laurel was on her knees in front of someone. I rushed over and saw Gabe lying on his back, foaming at the mouth.

"What's wrong with him?"

Laurel looked scared. "I don't know. What should we do?"

"Let's roll him over so he doesn't choke. We'd better call 9-1-1," I said.

"I'm already on it." I looked back and saw Fran behind us. In the excitement, I never noticed her.

I overheard Fran on the phone giving our location while Laurel and I rolled Gabe onto his side. As I steadied Gabe to make sure he wouldn't fall again, Laurel shoved her finger in his mouth, wiggled it around, and removed it quickly.

Her quick action amazed me. "That was gross," I said.

Laurel shrugged. "I wanted to make sure there are no obstructions. It wouldn't do much good to have him on his side if he is choking on his tongue."

"That's a good point."

Fran hung up and stood over us. "Ambulance is on the way." She looked around like she should do something, couldn't decide what that something was, then stepped backward to give us room.

I looked up at her. "What happened to him?"

"I'm not sure. We were both on the bus. I was in the front parlor reading a magazine, and he was in his room. Next thing that happened, he screamed and ran past me, right off the bus. I followed him out. He grabbed his head and ran around until he ran headfirst into your bus. Then he dropped to the ground there."

"Is there anything else we can do?" I asked.

Laurel grabbed Gabe's wrist and felt for a pulse. After thirty seconds of stillness, she let go. "Pulse is erratic. Fran, do you know if he took anything?"

Fran shook her head. "Like I said, he was in his room."

"Do you know where Russell is?"

"No. He's not here. I think he headed to town about an hour ago."

Off in the distance, I heard sirens, which was a good sign for Gabe. A couple of minutes later, an ambulance and a sheriff's car pulled up next to the bus. Fran and I both moved away to give the experts more room. Laurel provided a brief recap of what happened, then joined us while the paramedics worked on Gabe.

I saw one start an intravenous line while the other checked Gabe's heart. They took as short of time as possible before they loaded Gabe onto a gurney, loaded the gurney into the ambulance, and drove off, sirens blaring.

"We should go to the hospital," Fran said.

"Hold on. I have a few questions for you first."

All three of us turned around at once and saw Deputy Marvin standing by his truck, notepad in hand. "Starting with all your names and what happened here."

Fran stepped toward him. "You have our names. You were literally just here a couple of days ago."

"I know. Sorry. New incident, new report. If you could give me your IDs, that would be great."

We split off to retrieve the requested documentation, then met back at the truck, where the deputy patiently waited for us. Once there, he asked for the details of Gabe's adventure. Fran provided most of the story, and Laurel and I contributed what information we could. It didn't take long to write up what he had, then he gave us a ride to the local hospital.

When we got there, it surprised me when we turned the corner into the waiting room and saw Russell already there, seated in a chair, thumbing through a magazine.

Fran spoke up first. "What are you doing here?"

Russell set the magazine down on the seat next to him. "Sheriff called me when they brought Gabe in. I've only been here like five minutes."

We all sat and waited. Fran picked up the magazine Russell had rejected while Russell fiddled with his phone. Laurel amused herself by watching the television news. The sound was off, but the closed captioning was on, so she read each of the stories as they ran by.

I spent that time watching the three of them. I expected that since they lived and worked together that there would be some interaction, but there was none. They could have been three strangers waiting for a report on three different people. They didn't speak to each other, and except for passing glances, they didn't look at each other.

After about an hour, a doctor appeared in the room. The doctor was a giant of a man, at least six feet tall, dark skin and eyes, black beard, bald head. At first look, he could have passed for a wrestler or a bouncer, but his white coat and the stethoscope hanging from one pocket said otherwise.

"Who's here for Gabe Galvin?"

Four hands shot up in the air at once.

The doctor stepped into the middle of the room and gave us

the report.

"Your friend had an overdose. Also suffered a minor seizure and a heart attack. We had to pump his stomach, but he's stabilized now. He'll have to stay overnight, perhaps two nights until we can release him."

"Do you know what he took?" I asked.

"Based on the stomach contents, some designer opiates. One of which was laced with a rat poison."

The doctor's pager went off. He checked it, then ran from the room.

I understood little about the drug trade, but I guessed rat poison wasn't a common additive. To me, at least, it made little sense to get someone dependent on a drug, only to turn around and kill them. That sure didn't help with repeat business. Somehow, I needed to get myself out of the room and back to my bus and see what was in that capsule I couldn't identify.

I got out of my chair and tried to pretend I was invisible, but somehow, it didn't work.

"Where are you going?"

I turned around. It was Russell who asked, although Fran and Laurel were looking at me too.

"I'm just going to the restroom. I'll be right back."

CHAPTER TEN

I had to use the restroom, so I didn't tell a lie, because I headed straight there. What I didn't mention was that I had no intention of going back to the waiting room, so once I finished washing my hands, I walked directly to the main exit. Once I stepped through the automatic doors, I realized I made a mistake. Other than walking, I had no way to get back to the park. Normally I wouldn't mind the hike, but I felt the uncomfortable pressing of time against me, so I needed to return as soon as possible.

From my back pocket, I pulled out my phone and searched for rideshare services. I hadn't asked which one Laurel used when we traveled to town the previous day, and I had too many choices, so the multiple options stumped me. I have to admit that my biggest failing as a person was the inability to fully grasp the magic of cellular technology, which, I understand, makes no sense. Even I didn't understand how I can sit down at my laptop and program background music for the band. With accompanying fully synchronized light shows, yet I couldn't order myself a taxi.

Frustrated, I shoved my phone back into my pocket and

stepped back inside and approached the desk receptionist.

"Hi. This is embarrassing, but I need a ride back to where I'm staying. Would you do me a favor and call one for me? I would do it myself, but my phone battery is dead," I said. Passing him a look, I tried to appear wiped out and pitiful, which wasn't far from the truth.

I expected some push back, or a question or two, or at the least a raised eyebrow, but I got none of those. The receptionist picked up his desk phone, dialed a number, had a ten second conversation, and hung up.

"Cab will be here in three minutes, right out front there."

I gave him my best smile. "Thank you. I appreciate it."

I returned to the front walk and waited. As I did, I kept looking behind me, expecting Laurel, Russell, or Fran to pop out of the building and ask where I planned on running off to, but luckily for me, no one did.

The seconds seemed to stretch on, but eventually I saw an old-fashioned yellow taxicab slow down and stop right next to me.

"Where to?" the driver asked as I slipped into the back seat.

I looked into the rear-view mirror and caught the guy's eyes. He was an older gentleman, in his early sixties at least, with salt-and-pepper hair. He wore a gray flat cap, and there was a pair of fuzzy dice hanging from the mirror. I wondered if I entered a time machine instead of a taxi.

"The county park. The one right outside of town."

He didn't pull off right away like I expected, instead he just stared at me. He probably thought I was taking him for a ride.

"My tour bus is there, so I'm headed back to pick it up."

My answer seemed acceptable, because he shifted the car into drive, and he sped away from the curb. Ten minutes later, the driver parked right next to the first bus he came to, which turned out to be Toby's. That seemed fine to me. I had it in me to handle the extra thirty feet.

"That'll be sixteen dollars even."

I thought it was a little expensive, but I handed him a twenty and didn't wait for the change. I climbed from the cab, walked to my bus, unlocked the door, and entered. My heart skipped a beat when I noticed the baggie of drugs sitting on the dinette, because I realized at that moment, I should have locked them away with Merle on board. Gibson, by definition, is a curious cat, but he has nowhere near the ability to get into as much stuff as Merle or Dolly. They were the reason we didn't leave food out and triple checked the cabinets. With the curious critters aboard, all of the hatches had to be battened.

I shoved the bag into my pocket, then I checked my room to make sure everything was okay. Gibson was sitting at the foot of my bed washing himself. When he spotted me, he passed me a glance that let me know he wasn't happy that Merle, who still slumbered on the pillow tower, had usurped his spot.

I stepped back outside and looked to check if anyone was around, but I was alone. I walked over to Toby's bus and wanted to climb aboard, but the door didn't open for me. Hoping to find something, anything, I checked the bus storage bays, but the only one unlocked was empty.

At the rear of the bus, my luck turned for the better. The wall panel that closed off the kitchen was open, so I had the entire area to explore. I had access to the fridge, a small sink, a pull-out grill, and several cabinets. Carefully, I snooped through everything. Sadly, I found nothing but cooking utensils, a drawer of spices, unbreakable dishes, and a few aprons and towels.

I slammed the last door closed, turned, and noticed the trash can had tipped over. Beside the can was a small mass of used paper plates and napkins, and trailing away from that on the far side of the bus was a trail of garbage leading into the woods. I followed the trail like a bloodhound, and just inside the tree line, I discovered the large, black garbage bag with a hole in it. Based on the hole's size, I suspected a larger critter had been in there, like a raccoon, possum, or coyote, and I hoped it wasn't Dolly.

Most of the foodstuff spread out on the ground away from the bag. I recognized remnants of the dinner we'd had the other night, including burger parts and plenty of coleslaw. I also recognized a banana peel, some coffee grounds, and a pancake with a single bite from it. What caught my eye was a small, bright yellow plastic package with a mouse on the front along with a giant red X and a skull. Although the top of the package looked zipper-sealed, there was a hole chewed through the bottom. I guessed some poor creature was going to have a bad day.

Not wanting to touch the pouch, I looked around me until I found a stick of suitable size. I shoved the stick into the chew hole, lifted it, and carried it back to Toby's bus, where I set it on the table. From the cabinet, I grabbed a dark blue melamine plate and placed it next to the pouch. I extracted some granules from the package and made a small pile of them on the plate. Then I took the capsule from my pocket, opened it, and dumped about half onto the plate next to the pile. I carefully closed the capsule and returned it to the bag and my pocket. Relying on the entirety of my high school chemistry experience, I compared the two small lumps of powder. I expected the capsule to be a mixture of drugs and poison, but it surprised me to see there was no difference between the pill pile and the package pile.

"Oh, boy," I said to myself.

I needed to keep the package, so I checked through all the cabinets and drawers to find something to store it in, but I found nothing. In a last-ditch effort, I opened the fridge and spotted a bunch of sliced carrot and celery sticks in a gallon-sized plastic bag. I assumed that would do nicely, so I dumped the vegetables onto the table, and replaced them with the rat poison package.

"Was your little science experiment successful?"

The voice startled me, so I let out a squeal as I jumped back. It was Tommy again.

"Why do you insist on always sneaking up on me?" I asked,

harshly.

"I don't sneak. You're just inattentive."

I took some offense to that remark, but I didn't comment on it. One thing my detective dad taught me was to always be well aware of my environment.

Tommy took a step toward me. "What do you have there?"

I adjusted my grip on the bag so it was as obscure as I could make it with my tiny hand. "I have a big bag of none of your business. What do you want?"

"I want to know what you have there."

Tommy stepped in and reached for the bag. As he did, he pushed me against the table. I took the table's corner right in the hip, and the jab of pain brought stars to my eyes.

"Let me go!" I screamed as loud as a banshee, but I'd have to do better than that to attract any attention in the empty park.

I held the poison as far away from my body as I could, but Tommy clawed at my arm, desperately trying to reach it. Although he was physically larger than me, he wasn't as strong as he looked. When he made another thrust forward to get the bag, I sidestepped, put my left foot behind his leg, and pushed him.

Tommy pinwheeled his arms to regain his balance, but it was too late for that. He fell at an awkward angle and screamed when his left elbow took on the full weight of his body when he hit the concrete parking lot. I watched him for a moment to see what he'd do, but he didn't get up. He just rolled over onto his butt and rubbed his elbow. The tough guy started crying. Not an ugly cry, but the tears were flowing.

"You witch!" he screamed. "You don't understand, and you'll ruin everything!"

I took a few steps backward to keep him in sight as I retreated toward my bus.

"Yeah! You'd better leave. Get out of here before things get super bad for you! Leave and stay away for good!" he yelled after me like a playground bully.

I took a few more steps and determined he wouldn't follow me. I turned around and ran back to the bus, climbed aboard, and locked the door behind me. I shoved the rat poison into the cabinet beneath the sink, washed and dried my hands, and rushed to my bedroom.

Neither Merle nor Gibson were on the bed, which was good. I kneeled on the floor, threw the bed blankets onto the top, and opened one of the under-bed drawers. This was the drawer that held my safe, and all my secrets. Well, not secrets exactly, just rather important paperwork like my birth certificate and passport, a few thousand dollars in cash, and Betty. Normally, I don't carry Betty around with me. Since there was a murder, an attempted murder, and a physical assault all within a couple of days, I decided it was time for a little self-protection.

I punched my six-digit code into the keypad, then pulled on the handle, but it didn't open. I closed my eyes, took a deep breath, and counted to ten to calm myself. When I opened my eyes, I punched in the code again, slower, and pulled the handle, and this time the door opened. I grabbed Betty and a clip of ammunition, closed the safe and the drawer, and smoothed the bed blankets back into place.

Once I had Betty, I grabbed her holster from a hook in the closet, put everything together, and strapped her on. Dad trained me how to use a gun and I wasn't afraid to carry one. That came as another advantage of having a detective father. He taught me how to shoot handguns and long guns when I was still in my early teens. He taught me how to use them, clean them, and respect them. I'd have to say I'm a pretty excellent shot, although I practice as little as possible. Sometimes when we have a down day, Bozeman and I will find a range and take turns practicing with his rifle, but those days are few and often far between.

One thing my father and I disagreed on was whether to shoot to kill or shoot to stop. He always told me that once I got to where I had to draw my weapon, the time for niceties was over. At that point, I needed to shoot to kill because the aggressor might overtake and disarm me. I told him he had a valid point, but I disagreed with him. I didn't want to take a life if I could help it, and that's why Betty only held non-lethal rounds. Also, she was only a .22 caliber, so with that, she was the biggest weapon I dared to carry. Yet I still felt protected. I doubt I would ever kill anyone if I shot them, but for sure I would give them a reason to let me be, especially if I did the double-tap dad trained me to do.

Armed, I snuck back out to the living area and looked out the window. I saw Toby's bus, but not the back end where I'd encountered Tommy. I didn't see him near Toby's bus, and I checked several other windows and didn't see him near mine, so I thought the coast was clear.

Against my leg, I sensed a nudge. I looked down and saw Merle head-butting my shin just above my ankle. That was his signal to me he was ready to leave the bus. I picked him up, scratched his head, and opened the door. Before I walked out, I looked left, right, and left again, just like I was crossing a street. Then, seeing no one, I stepped into the parking lot. Tommy wouldn't realize I was now armed, but I hoped that if he saw me, a skunk would be enough of a deterrent to leave me be.

Merle twitched in my arms, so I set him down and watched him scamper away. I could tell it was time for him to do his business, and I was happy to let him. Although I trained Dolly to use Gibson's litter box, Merle couldn't pick up that skill.

Thinking of Dolly, I needed to check on her to make sure she was safe and sound. The last thing I wanted to learn was that she was the one who ate through the rat poison package in the woods. Still on high alert, I checked the area as I walked to Dolly's compartment. The door was open, which was the standard when we parked, and I looked in and saw Dolly's pretty black eyes staring back at me.

"Hello, Dolly," I whispered.

Dolly stretched like a cat, then moved toward the door. When she was close enough, I picked her up and scratched her head. In response, she climbed higher up my chest, and put both paws over my left shoulder and set her chin down. In that position, she looked like a big hairy baby waiting to be burped, but it was actually a demand to give her back a good scratching, which I happily did.

As I gave Dolly her scratches, I walked around the bus, looking out for Tommy. There was no sign of him, so I walked over and looked around Toby's bus as well. Tommy wasn't anywhere around there, either.

I spotted the trash can and realized I needed to clean that mess up. If it was one thing I believed in, it was being a good steward of the environment. I carried Dolly back to my bus, set her on the ground, and opened the compartment where we kept our maintenance supplies. From there, I grabbed a pair of gardening gloves and a large black trash bag.

I put on the gloves and carried the bag into the woods, where I dumped the other trash bag into mine. Then I collected all the litter in the area and cleaned up the trash trail that led from the bus to the woods. Back at Toby's bus, I threw away the melamine plate holding the rat poison, and all the paper products. The celery and carrot sticks I gathered up and threw into the woods. The local animals could eat those. Once I gathered all the trash, I closed the bag, put a knot on the top and set it inside the trash can. The trash can had clamps on the side to hold the lid on, although I imagined any smart animal could get past that. But I was too tired to haul the bag over to the dumpster the park provided. Instead, I returned to my bus, put everything away, and set up my chair.

I thought about getting a book or something to drink when I saw a flash of gray fur run past my feet, followed closely behind by a flash of black and white. Instead of moving, I sat still and watched Merle and Dolly play. They had this weird game they played, which seemed to be a combination of tag and hide and go seek. One would chase the other, and tackle them once they caught them, then they'd switch, and the pursuer would become the pursued. It was fun to watch, but I never wanted to play. Too much running for my taste.

I heard a car approach, so I leaned over so I could see better. It was a green sedan, and it pulled up and Laurel got out of the back seat.

"There you are. I thought you were going to the restroom," Laurel said with more relief in her voice than disappointment.

"I did. Get yourself a chair and sit down."

Laurel found a chair, unfolded it, put it next to mine, and settled into it. We were sitting with our backs to the sun, and the rays felt warm and comforting on my shoulders.

"What are you doing here?" she asked.

"Babysitting."

As soon as I uttered the words, Merle popped out from behind a tire, did a full circle around Laurel's feet, and ran under the bus. On instinct, rather than out of fear, Laurel picked up her feet. A few seconds later, Dolly raced by, backtracked, and sat down right in front of us.

"He went that way." I cocked a thumb in the direction Merle went. Dolly looked at me, then headed in the general area to which I pointed. The encounter was priceless, and Laurel and I laughed. It felt good to laugh.

"How's Gabe doing?" I asked.

"The doctor says he's going to need to stay in the hospital for a couple of days. By the time I left, we still didn't have any details of the drugs he took, so I have no clue if they were uppers, or downers, or what."

"I'm more interested in the rat poison. I found a package in the trash near your bus. Then I compared it to the contents of that capsule you gave me, and it looked the same to me. Do you know anything about that?"

"What? No. Of course not. I didn't know we had anything like that on the bus. Why would we? I've never seen a single sign of rodents aboard."

I nodded. "It would have taken time to fill those capsules, and you saw no one doing anything like that?"

"No. I think I'd not only notice something like that, but I'd certainly question it."

I looked over at Laurel. "We need to get the rest of those drugs and turn them over to the police. Hopefully, they'll have a way to identify them."

"Perhaps they could get fingerprints off the pills."

I doubted that could be done, but I didn't want to say otherwise. "Maybe. Hey, you've got a visitor."

Laurel looked at the ground. Merle was sitting at her feet.

"He wants some attention. Pick him up if you want to."

Laurel grinned and didn't hesitate. Within seconds, she had Merle on her lap and was stroking his fur. "You're such a pretty boy, aren't you?"

"Do you know Tommy Skye?" I asked.

Laurel nodded. "Not formally, but I know of him. Why?"

"He's been lurking around here the last couple of days. I had an encounter with him earlier. He seems intent on running me off and out of the park."

Laurel's eyes widened. "Are you okay?"

"I'm fine. He got more banged up than I did. I just wanted you to know that he's out here somewhere. And based on the way he shows up at the most inopportune moments, he's probably camped out on the edge of the woods somewhere."

"Okay. But why?" she asked.

I shook my head. "You tell me. I don't know what he's doing here. He told me he lives in Los Angeles."

Laurel moved to place Merle back on the ground. "I'd better go get those drugs before Fran and Russell get here. They should be back soon."

"Do you have the bus key?" I asked.

Laurel thought for a second. "Actually, no, I don't."

"Then you can stay where you are and cuddle with the skunk. The door's locked."

Laurel exhaled in frustration. "It sure would be nice to be treated like an adult and part of the team."

"Sorry, but the team's about to be over. Y'all were here for Toby. Toby's gone now, so then, so is the band."

Laurel frowned. "With all that's been going on, I haven't even thought about that. I guess I won't need a key after all."

"Have you thought at all about what you're going to do next?"

Laurel shook her head. "Not a single thought. I don't know. Maybe I'll go spend time with my grandmother, although I really do like being out on the road and playing for people."

"I agree. There's nothing like it in all the world, being up on that stage and having all those people listening to your music."

Laurel smiled. "Well, I'm not worried. There's always a band looking for a good fiddle player, right? And if that doesn't work out, I can always switch back to classical and join an orchestra somewhere."

"I'll bet you could. Before you go, I need your help with just one simple thing."

"Sure. What is it?"

"Help me get Bozeman out of jail and back home."

CHAPTER ELEVEN

Dolly noticed Merle was getting all the attention, and couldn't have that, so she climbed up the side of my chair and plopped right down in my lap. She nuzzled at my hand until I scratched her nose right between the eyes. Afterward, I worked on her ears, and she relaxed, and I felt her go limp. I knew from experience if I kept it up, I'd have a raccoon sleeping on my lap within five minutes.

"What's our next move?" Laurel asked.

I glanced over at Laurel, who was still playing with Merle. Normally, the kids were shy around strangers, but they both took to Laurel like bees to clover. "Well, I'd like to get Gabe's drugs and turn them over to the cops, and I'd love the chance to search his room. Too late, though. It looks like the rest are back."

When the Ford van pulled up, the brakes squealed in a pitch that assaulted my ears. It must have been twice as bad on Merle and Dolly because they both jumped from our laps and scurried toward their nest.

I watched as a man whom I had never seen before stepped out of the passenger seat. He looked to be as average as a man could be. Average height, light brown hair, and a runner's build with the beginning of a rounded stomach. Unlike Laurel and I, who dressed in jeans T-shirts, the man was wearing black dress slacks, a white button-down shirt, and a skinny black tie.

He must have recognized Laurel because he walked right over to us.

"Hey, Steve. This is my friend, Codi Cassidy. Codi, this is Steve Ridgeway. He's the bus driver. Are we leaving soon? We must be if you're back."

Steve shook my hand when I offered it. He had a firm, but not overpowering, grip. "Nice to meet you. Yeah, I got a call from the record company. We'll be shoving off today."

"Hey, Steve, can I have the key? I need a jacket, and they locked the bus, and I'm the only one here."

Without comment, Steve fished a key ring from his pocket, picked through until he found the right one, and held it out for Laurel.

"Here. Put them in the driver's seat when you get in."

Laurel took the keys and smiled. "Thanks, Steve. Keep Codi company until I get back, will you? She doesn't like to be alone."

Laurel got up and Steve replaced her in the chair. For a few moments, we looked at each other like we were on an awkward first date.

"So, you're a musician too?" he asked.

I smiled. "Yes. You've heard of me? Are you a fan?"

"No. I saw your name written on the side of your bus there."

Talk about deflating someone's ego. I took my turn at the unpleasant conversation. "So how long have you been Toby's driver?"

Steve stared at me for a second, and I guessed that he wouldn't answer, and at worst he would walk away, but he leaned back in the chair and crossed his legs. "Oh, I don't know for sure. Three, perhaps three and a half years."

"Driving is hard work. I always feel bad for Bozeman. He's

my partner, and he has to drive this hunk of metal around."

Steve didn't comment.

"Laurel told me you don't stay on the bus when you get to a location. Why is that?"

"Why do you care?" he asked.

That question seemed to raise his dander. "I don't, really. Only thought it was unusual. I thought drivers always stayed on the bus."

Steve uncrossed his legs. He noticed a small rock near his right foot. He kicked at it, and it skittered under my bus.

"Toby and I have an arrangement. I take care of other areas of his business, so I stay off site so I can concentrate on it without all the distractions that go on around the bus."

"That's interesting. I thought Russell as the band manager handled all of Toby's business affairs."

Steve glared at me for a moment and rose. "Nice meeting you, Codi Cassidy. Have a nice day." He said the 'have a nice day part' so cold and sarcastic that the words still hung in midair as he turned and walked to Toby's bus. I hoped Laurel had finished whatever she was doing in there, because she'd been gone too long to have simply gone for a jacket.

Steve stepped onto the bus and disappeared from sight. I pledged to wait only five minutes for Laurel to come out, and if she didn't return by that time, I would go over and find her myself. I pulled my phone from my back pocket, found the timer feature, set it for five minutes, and pressed the little green button. For a couple of seconds, I watched the numbers flip to make sure it was running and turned my attention to the bus. I waited. Five minutes dropped to four. Four eventually became three. After what seemed to be an hour, three turned to two, then finally to one. My eyes darted from the phone to the bus as the last minute ticked away.

The alarm rang, and I fumbled for the button to shut it off. Once my phone was silent, I got to my feet and started walking toward the bus. I reached a little over halfway when Laurel bounded down the steps and skipped off in my direction.

She was wearing a bright yellow raincoat that looked to be at least one size too big for her. She looked, in a word, ridiculous, especially considering there wasn't a single rain cloud to be seen in the big blue sky.

"Come on." She interlocked her elbow into mine, spun me around, and escorted me back aboard my bus. There, she removed the raincoat. "Did he follow us?"

I looked out the door and the parlor window. "Nope. I don't think so."

"Why are you wearing that coat? It looks silly on you."

"It protects me from the rain," she answered matter-of-factly.

"But it's not raining out."

"Oh, I also love it because it has lots of internal pockets to protect other things from the rain and from spying eyes."

Laurel picked up the coat and rummaged around inside. "I've got some presents for you."

She handed me what looked to be a pill bottle. The bottle label said it was a generic multi-vitamin, but I could tell right away the label was fake because someone had misspelled the word vitamin. I twisted open the top, tipped over the bottle, and a few of the pills I hadn't been able to identify tumbled into my palm.

"Thanks. That's what I've always wanted."

"Wait. There's more," Laurel said.

Laurel reached back into her coat and removed a baggie. In it were over a dozen of the tainted capsules.

"Nice. Those were in that fake book you told me about?"

"Yep. And that fake book got me thinking. If he had one item like that to hide stuff in, maybe he would have more. So…"

Laurel dipped into her coat for a third time and extracted a yellow legal pad. She handed it to me and sat back in the captain's chair. "Last present. Good things come in threes."

I took the pad and looked at it. The first page had doodles. Nothing artistic, only random lines, boxes, triangles. I flipped the first page over, and the second page was the same, except the sketches seemed to be someone's initial attempt at artwork.

"What is this?" I asked.

"To me, it looked like he was trying to come up with a personal or band logo, and not doing a good job at it."

I looked at it again with that in mind, and some images kind of made sense in that respect. The lines I'd mistaken as scribble lines now resembled drumsticks, at least a little. I wasn't sure what Gabe was going for, but he convinced me if he really wanted his own logo, he should ask a graphic designer or someone at the record company about it. Drawing was not in his wheelhouse.

"Why am I looking at these?" I asked.

"Keep turning the pages," Laurel said.

I flipped to the next page and found a list of songs. I looked up at Laurel. "Toby's set list?"

"Not in order. Just some of the common songs we'd play during a show. Some we always play aren't on there, and there are a couple included we haven't played in forever."

"Where did you find this?"

"There was a false bottom in one of his drawers. In there was a dirty magazine, and this. Please, keep going."

I turned the page, and this got my attention. It was a block of text, written in block letters. After I cleared my throat, I read them aloud to get their full effect.

"I don't know why I'm here. I hate them all. Why can't I leave? I hate Fran, always flaunting her sex like a peacock in heat and flashing her boobs at every opportunity. I hate Laurel and her oh, shucks, look at me I'm a down-home country girl who's so innocent."

My eyes slid from the page, and I looked at Laurel.

She smiled and shrugged. "Well, I guess he doesn't like me."

I turned back to the note. "I hate Toby. He walks around like he's God's gift to country music with his stupid sequined jackets and his flashy boots. If people learned the things I did about him, he wouldn't be able to serve beer at a country bar, let alone be a country star. If it wasn't for Billy running his mic through the computer, he'd sound like an old goat chewing on a tin can. Who's Billy?"

"He's the lead sound engineer," Laurel said. She got up, crossed to the pantry, and helped herself to a bottle of water. She brought me one, too.

"Is this part true about Toby's singing?"

"Well, I am under an NDA, but I will tell you that Toby would never get confused with Frank Sinatra. And you know all those singers who have a unique voice? Willie Nelson? Kenny Rogers? Bob Dylan?"

"Yeah, of course. I named one of my chipmunks after Willie."

"Well, they would never consider Toby in that class, either."

"So, you're saying he's a fake? The computer Gabe mentions. Is it voice modulation or pitch correction?"

"Both." Laurel held her hands up in front of her. "You didn't hear me say anything of the sort, now did you?"

I let it drop and returned to the note. "The world needs to learn the truth, and I think I should be the one to tell them. I will destroy him for what he did to me. Well, that got cryptic quick, didn't it?"

Laurel nodded. "Yeah. It had a strong start, especially that part about Fran, but it lost its steam after a few sentences. Not bad for a manifesto start, though."

I flipped to the next one. It was blank, so I closed the book and offered it to Laurel.

Laurel refused to take it. "No. You missed the best part.

Keep going."

I took it back and paged through it again. After a few blank pages, I found the real prize. "Holy moly. It's Bozeman's song."

I removed the two sheets of paper from the pad and put them on the dinette table like they were museum exhibits. I grabbed Toby's sheet music from the counter and handed it to Laurel.

"Here. You compare the two and tell me what you think."

Laurel took her time and compared Toby's song to Bozeman's. After five minutes, she set the paper down on the table. "Except for the title and a couple of word changes, it's exactly the same."

"Did you check the dates?" I asked.

Laurel picked the paper back up, found the music copyright date, and compared it to the hand-scrawled date on Bozeman's page. "It looks like Bozeman's is a good ten years earlier. What are you going to do now that you have this back?"

"I don't know for sure. I might get Bozeman's lawyer looped in and see what she says. Hypothetically, of course. Excuse me."

While I trusted Laurel, I didn't want to include her in my conversation with Bozeman's lawyer. So, she waited where she was while I went into my bedroom and made the call. It didn't take long for us to come up with a game plan.

I returned to the other room.

"Well?" Laurel asked.

"Hold on." With my phone, I took pictures of everything Laurel had brought me. I snapped photos of every page on the legal pad, as well as Bozeman's handwritten lyrics and the sheet music. "She recommends we turn everything over to Sheriff Cross."

"Is that really a good idea?"

"I asked that same question. Bozeman's lawyer said yes, though. The lawyer won't be able to use the evidence at the arraignment hearing. But she might use it to persuade the district attorney that Bozeman isn't the killer. I want to make one stop first."

Rather than put everything back in Laurel's raincoat, I instead found a brown paper grocery bag that fit everything nicely. We got off the bus just in time to see Fran and Russell exit a ride share car. I jogged over to the driver's window.

"Hey, can you take my friend and I to a couple places?"

The driver checked his phone to see if he had anyone already slated. "You're good. Get in."

I climbed into the seat behind the driver, but as Laurel reached for the handle of the other back door, Russell grabbed her arm.

"Where are you going?" He sneered.

Laurel looked over at me, then back at Russell. "I'm just going back to check on Gabe."

"You can't. We're leaving. Right now."

"You know as well as I do it will take at least an hour for Steve to get everything cleaned up and ready to go. Just give us an hour, okay? If I'm not back by then, you can leave without me."

Russell let go of her wrist and opened the door for her. "I'll be generous. Two hours. No more."

Laurel climbed in and Russell slammed the door behind her. "We don't have a lot of time."

I nodded, then instructed the driver to take us to the county hospital. I told the truth when I said I would turn it over to the sheriff. Forgetful me, I didn't mention I wanted to have one last conversation with Gabe about it first.

We arrived at the hospital and found our way to Gabe's room. When we approached, the door was closed, and Laurel took the lead and opened it a crack. I could see the lights were out, but the random flicker told us the television was on.

"Gabe? Are you awake?" Laurel said, just above a whisper.

"Who's there?"

"It's me, Laurel. Codi is here to see you, too. Can we come in?"

There was a delayed answer. "I suppose."

Laurel opened the door wide, and we entered the room. There were two chairs nearby, one on either side of the bed, so we each took a seat.

I knew Laurel had little time, so I got right into it. "Gabe, can you tell me about the drugs?"

"What drugs?"

I fished the bottle out of the bag and held it out. The TV didn't cast enough light, so Gabe pressed a button, and an over-bed light came on. I shook that bottle in front of him. The pills rattled inside.

"Those aren't mine," he said.

Laurel leaned over to Gabe. "I found them in your room, Gabe. And the doctor said they pumped those same types of pills from your stomach. You want to stick with the 'you never saw them before' story?"

Gabe looked at Laurel, at me, then back at her.

"Okay. Look, you don't understand the pressure I'm under. They help keep me balanced, you know? Mellow. Attentive. I'm only doing them for the good of the band. For Toby and the rest of you."

I fished out the baggie and held it before his eyes. "What are these supposed to do?"

Gabe looked at the capsules briefly, then stared at the television. There was a baseball game on with the sound turned down. "He told me those would help me sleep."

"Who's he? Who gave these to you?"

Gabe shook his head. "I can't tell you that."

"Did you know what's in these? Rat poison. Your doctor confirmed it, and I found the package in the trash can on your bus. Whoever you're trying to protect gave you rat poison. Sure, those will help you sleep, especially if your intention is to sleep forever."

Gabe focused on me again. "You're trying to trick me. I'm never going to tell you."

"You want to tell us about this, then?" I put the drugs back in the paper bag and pulled out the legal pad.

"Where did you get that?"

Laurel spoke up. "I found it in your secret drawer with your copy of Boob Monthly. You saying this isn't yours, either?"

Laurel reached over, grabbed the pad from my hand, and turned to the second page. "Are you saying you didn't do this? You're not trying to design a logo for your bass drum? Thinking about starting your own band?"

Gabe reached up and ran his fingers along the page. "No. This pad is mine. I just haven't seen it in a long time. A few weeks ago, I lost it. I'm just surprised you found it. Why would you even care? It's just a stupid logo."

"We don't give a toot about the logo. We care about your manifesto."

"What are you talking about?" he asked.

Laurel flipped to the correct spot and read it to him. As she read, I watched Gabe's face for any micro-expressions. The only one I noticed was a general look of confusion that anyone could see.

"Let me see that," Gabe said.

Laurel handed him the pad, and Gabe studied it. "I didn't write this. I wrote none of these things."

"Come on, Gabe. Fess up," Laurel said.

"No. Okay, I'll admit that those drugs were mine. I can't deny that. But this I didn't do."

"We don't believe you, Gabe," I said.

Laurel and I hadn't considered doing the good-musician, bad-musician routine on him, but it seemed to work.

"Look, watch, bring that tray closer."

I looked where Gabe was pointing and saw an adjustable bedside table. I wheeled it over and put it over the bed so Gabe had full access to it. On the table was a pen and a crossword puzzle book that someone had brought him to help ward off boredom. Crosswords must not have been his thing, though, because the puzzle the book was open to only had five words filled in. I could tell just with a glance that the answers to two questions were wrong.

"Give me a sheet of paper."

Laurel looked at me for approval, and when I nodded, she tore the last page from the legal pad and set it on the table.

Gabe picked up the pen. "Okay, now read me the note again."

Laurel read, and Gabe wrote what she said.

I noticed something was off right away. "Hold it. Gabe, you're writing in cursive. Do block letters, like in the note."

Gabe crossed out what he had written. "Sorry. Let's do it over. Anytime you're ready, Laurel."

Laurel read the note again, this time slower, because it took Gabe longer to write in the same style of the note. Laurel got through three sentences before I stopped her and asked for the pad.

I set the pad on the table and placed Gabe's version right next to it. At first, I only scanned it, then went back and read it with more intention and I compared them one letter at a time.

I looked at Gabe, then at Laurel. "He didn't write this note."

"How can you tell?"

"Get closer and look. Not even close to being the same," I said.

"Maybe he faked his handwriting when he wrote it just now," Laurel argued.

"He could have, but I don't think so. There are too many discrepancies in the way he wrote the letters."

"Good. Does that mean I'm off the hook, then?" Gabe asked.

"Not yet. I've got one more question. Have you ever seen this before?" I removed Bozeman's song from the pad and placed it on the table.

Gabe leaned forward and was about to grab it when I stopped him. "No. Don't touch it."

Gabe removed his hand from the area and instead looked at the document where it lay. "No. I've never seen this before."

I put the song back where it was and returned everything to the bag. "Gabe, I'm sorry we disturbed you. I really hope you feel better soon."

Laurel and I stood and left, leaving Gabe to his baseball game.

"Well? What do you think?" Laurel asked.

"I think Gabe's an addict, but that's about it. Come on, let's go find the sheriff."

Laurel and I jumped into the waiting car, and the driver took us to the sheriff's office. Laurel waited in the car while I stepped inside to visit Sheriff Cross.

The desk officer escorted me to Cross's office, which was open. I knocked on the door just to be polite, entered, and sat down in the leather guest chair in front of his desk without being asked.

The sheriff was in the middle of typing out a report when I entered, but he turned his attention from the computer to me.

"What can I do for you, Ms. Cassidy?"

"I have a few items here that Bozeman's attorney asked me to turn in."

I opened the bag and lined up the pill bottle, bag of capsules, the pad, and Bozeman's lyrics on his desk, then explained the significance of each.

He seemed especially interested in the drugs, but not so much in the notepad or Bozeman's song. To his credit, though, he put each of the items into its own evidence bag and labeled everything with Bozeman's case number.

Nothing more needed to be said, so I rejoined Laurel, and we rode together to the park. Once we were out of the car, Laurel came over and gave me a hug.

"I guess I'll be shoving off soon. It was such a pleasure to meet you, Codi. I hope Bozeman gets out of jail, and you two can get back to a normal life."

I smiled. "Thanks, Laurel. I appreciate it. I wish you well on whatever it is you do next."

Laurel let go of me, and I watched her walk away.

CHAPTER TWELVE

When Laurel left, I took a seat and placed my head in my hands. I wanted to cry, but I wouldn't. I wasn't about to descend into that pit of misery, although I was in the mood to feel sorry for myself. Here I was, sitting all alone, but then I remembered Bozeman sitting all alone in the slammer. At least I had my freedom.

I couldn't understand where I got it wrong. All signs pointed directly at Gabe as the killer, but those signs were mistaken. I considered what to do next. Clean the bus? Practice my guitar? Wallow in self-pity? None of the options seemed like good ones.

At that moment, I remembered Laurel's garish yellow raincoat that she'd left with me. Not wanting her to go without it, I stepped onto the bus to get it. When I leaned across the dinette to pick up the coat, something caught my eye outside the window, or rather, someone.

My eyes followed Tommy as he crept out of the tree line near my bus. He didn't even glance in my direction, and seemed interested in Toby's bus, not mine. He disappeared from view, so I quickly repositioned myself near the driver's seat. From there, I watched as he picked his way to the other bus.

Once at the bus, he crouched down and rolled under. As I watched, a bundle flew out from beneath the bus, and a second later, another followed. After a moment, Tommy's leg popped out, followed by the rest of him. He hesitated, took a tentative look around and picked up both bundles and scampered away. I noticed he followed the same path as the trash I picked up earlier. This piqued my interest, so I placed Laurel's rain jacket on the driver's seat and left the bus.

I sprinted to Toby's bus and flattened myself against the side so no one would spot me through any of the windows. Slowly, I made my way to the rear and peeked around the corner to ensure no one was by the outdoor kitchen. The coast seemed clear, so I ran to the woods where I'd seen Tommy enter.

Once in the trees, I stopped, looked around, and remembering Tommy's earlier threat, took Betty from the holster and clicked off the safety. I found a deer path that I followed for a few yards and soon came to a junction. I had a decision to make. Left or right. Since he'd come out of the woods near my bus, I turned right and walked along the trail. Off in the distance, I overheard voices, so I slowed my gait.

Fifty feet later, I walked around a bend and stopped. Up ahead, kneeling on the ground facing away from me, I found Tommy. The voices I'd picked up came from a small radio, and the two bundles he'd taken occupied Tommy's attention. I took a few silent steps forward, and I realized the bundles were pillowcases, and from one, Tommy was removing canned goods.

"You progressed from playing guitar to stealing food?" I asked. I hoped my voice didn't shake out loud like it did in my head.

Tommy turned so quickly he lost his balance and fell flat on his behind. He looked like he wanted to pounce but spotted my firearm and settled back in his seat.

I waved the gun at the food. "What's going on here?"

He looked at the can of soup he held in his hand and returned it to the pillowcase. "This isn't what you think."

"Not what I think? So, then I didn't just witness you sneak over to his bus and steal this stuff. What is all this, anyway? How did you get on the bus?"

"I didn't."

"Why lie to me? It's only going to make things worse for you."

Tommy brushed his hands on his pants. "There's a maintenance panel near the back. It opens up into Toby's bedroom."

That made me wonder about the security of my bus, and Tommy read me like we were sitting around playing poker.

"Don't worry about that. Your bus is too old. It doesn't have that same design."

"Why did you break into Toby's bus? For food? You expect me to accept that? I thought you live in L.A."

"I do. There are some things you don't understand," he said.

I thought I understood fine, but if he wanted to talk, I'd let him go. "Why don't you explain it all to me? What brought you here?"

I could tell he didn't want to talk to me, so I motioned with the gun to implore him to continue the story.

"Things haven't been going well for me, and I've been down on my luck. I used the last of my money to drive out here to see Toby."

"Where's your car? There's no one else in the parking lot."

"The old clunker broke down as I got into town. I kept it going until I got it to the garage, then I walked the rest of the way here."

"Why did you want to see Toby?"

"Because. I wanted to ask for a loan, you know, for old

time's sake. I thought he'd do that for me, especially for the way he screwed me over by replacing me with Fran." Tommy shifted in his seat. He put his hand under his backside and tossed an uncomfortable rock into the trees.

"Interesting. Did you talk to him?" I asked.

Tommy took a sudden interest in the ground. He found a stick, picked it up, and started drawing patterns in the dirt.

"Tommy? Did you talk to Toby? Tell me the truth."

"Yes, I did. After the sound check, I followed him back to the bus."

"What happened?"

"I asked him to give me a loan. He seemed already angry, so he said no."

"Then you got mad and strangled him and shoved a song down his throat?" I asked. There was no way to cushion that question.

"No. Of course not, no" Tommy raised his stick, but because it was only the size of a magic wand, it seemed more cute than threatening. "I never touched him that way. I couldn't."

"But I'll bet you wanted to," I said.

Tommy dropped the stick. "Of course I wanted to. Ever since I was a young boy, I wanted to be in a band, so I worked hard to make that happen. Do you know what a distinguished career I had? How many albums I've been on? How many stars I've played with? I've toured with country music royalty, and Toby took all that away when he traded me in for that woman. I admit, I would've loved to kill him, but I didn't."

"Someone told me it was your own fault you got kicked out. Missing rehearsals, talk of you doing drugs, that sort of behavior."

I saw him getting agitated, but regardless of how much he got worked up, he didn't make a move toward me.

"Hey, I'm telling you, I did not murder Toby. I couldn't have."

"Are you sure?" He seemed sure, but I wanted to see it in his eyes when he denied it.

"Yes. I never even stepped on the bus. There's no way I could have strangled him on the ground and carried him on the bus. I'm not strong enough,"

"What do you mean?"

Tommy retrieved his stick and retraced the patterns he already drew in the dirt. "I'm ill. Chronically. I've only got a couple of months left to live."

His body language told me he spoke the truth.

"I'm sorry." His confession hit me in the heart, and I lowered Betty to my side. I kept the safety off. I can be sympathetic without being stupid.

He smiled. "Thanks. I appreciate it."

"Toby knew?"

"Of course. That's why I missed rehearsals. And the medications they had me on initially only made it worse. They kept me in a half-comatose state most of the time. Those first days were so hard on me. Physically and mentally."

"And your long-time friend turned his back on you, and rather than help, he cut you loose."

Tommy nodded.

"Nice guy," I said.

Tommy nodded again and threw his stick into the brush. "Yeah, tell me about it."

"So, why are you stealing?" I asked.

Tommy shrugged. "I'm hungry. And like I said, with my car in the shop, I can't get back to Los Angeles, anyway. Once Toby got killed, the bus stayed empty most of the time, so I dropped in when I noticed no one around and took whatever supplies I needed."

"Show me your treasure."

Tommy hesitated, then grabbed the first pillowcase and tipped it upside-down. I watched as canned goods, a head of lettuce, two bananas, and an orange tumbled out. The other pillowcase held a blue melamine plate, a steak knife, two spoons, and a fork.

I nodded, and Tommy gathered up the items and placed them back into the cases.

"Are you going to turn me in?" he asked.

"I should. You're a thief. But no. I don't think I will, as long as you answer one more question for me."

"Sure. What is it?"

"Do you do drugs?"

"Like I said, I'm terminal. I eat dinner with the Grim Reaper at the table every night. Of course I do drugs. Mostly pain killers."

"I meant illegals. Street stuff."

"No. I admit, I tried cocaine once, but I hated the way it made me feel afterward, and I never did it again. Also, I had the unpleasant opportunity to see firsthand what they did to a lot of good people. I always avoided illegal drugs like the plague."

"Ever sell them?"

"Nope. I never got into that, either. Hell, I never even got much into liquor."

I stared at him for a few moments, satisfied he was being honest with me.

"Do you need anything out here?" I asked.

Russell shook his head. "No. With this haul, I'm good for a few days."

"Where have you been sleeping?"

"I don't really sleep much, but when I need to, I either nap on the bench in the locker room or go over to the bleachers."

"Look, I'd like to invite you on the bus, but I'm all alone on there."

Tommy nodded. "Sure, I understand."

"You didn't let me finish. I have a lounge lawn chair I will put out next to the bus, and I'll put a blanket out there too, okay?"

"I'd appreciate that. Thank you."

I tucked Betty back into her holster and gave Tommy a tentative wave goodbye and turned to leave.

Tommy stopped me. "Hey."

I turned back around to face him.

"Take the first trail you find on your left. It'll take you right back to your bus."

"Thanks."

I left Tommy with his treasures and walked back to my bus. Once there, I trudged once more up the bus steps, and ran right into Laurel, who stood there waiting for me.

"Where have you been? Get in here."

I accepted Laurel's invitation to enter my personal domicile and threw myself into the first chair I came to.

"What's up? I thought you guys had an itching to leave," I said.

"We are soon, but I found something I need you to look at."

Parched, I rose from my chair, headed to the storage room, grabbed a couple of bottles of water, and headed back for my chair. On the way, I passed one bottle to Laurel. I opened mine and drank half the contents before I returned my attention to my visitor.

"What do you need to show me?"

Laurel thrust her phone at me, so I took it and looked at the screen.

"What is this?" I expanded the view on the screen to make it bigger and examined the picture. I had to keep moving the image on the screen to read it normally, but I got the gist quick. "Holy cow, is this a life insurance policy? Where did you find this?"

"Russell's room."

I read the page more. The insured was Toby Madden, and the beneficiary was a trust, and I could only guess who headed that trust. The policy paid two million dollars. I read the fine print and discovered the double indemnity clause I assumed I'd find there.

I held up the phone. "Do you know what you found here?"

"I do if you mean a motive to kill off Toby?"

I nodded. "If what you say is true, and Toby wasn't the best of singers, maybe his act was over-inflated. What about this scenario? Russell knew that Toby's star had limited reach. Between his lacking vocal abilities and his over-bearing personality, Toby would end up playing at dirty bars and supermarket openings. So, rather than lose all the money, Russell kills him off."

"It sounds plausible to me, and four million bucks is an excellent motive. Of course, you don't know for sure who that trust is for. For all you know, all the money goes to homeless, hungry children," Laurel said.

I nodded. "That's fair. Point taken. Any chance you have more pictures in here that would show that?"

"I had little time, so I was lucky to grab these pictures."

"Where did you find this in Russell's room?"

"Well, I got to thinking about that false bottom in Gabe's room, and I wondered if everyone had those secret hiding spaces. Toby had a false bottom in his closet, but I found it empty."

"Wait, did it look like it was always empty, like Toby never knew it existed? Or did it look like he stored something there at one point, but someone removed whatever Russell had there?"

"I don't know. I didn't stay long enough to get into that kind of detail. Once I saw nothing in it, I moved on."

"Did you find other hidden compartments in Toby's room?"

"No, but that doesn't mean there aren't any. So back to where I found this, in a false bottom of his bottom dresser drawer."

"Did you spot anything else in there?"

"Actually, yes. He filled the drawer with documents, but I thought I heard someone coming, so I snapped this picture, closed it back up again, and left. Did I do okay?"

I grinned at her. "You did great. Now, do you think you can do me one more favor?"

It took about fifteen minutes to explain my plan, then Laurel grabbed her raincoat and left me. While I waited for Laurel to implement the secret plan, I headed outside and pulled the chaise from the compartment. I set it up near the front bumper on the passenger side, so it would hide Tommy from view as much as possible. Then I rummaged around inside until I found a blanket and a small travel pillow, then added a couple of bottles of water to the pile in my arms. I carried it all outside and set everything on the chair.

When that task was complete, I wanted to check on all the kids. It was getting close to dinnertime, so Willie and Waylon had already returned to their nest for the night. I closed the little chicken-wire gate we used to keep them safe at night and during travel times.

Next, I checked on Merle and Dolly. Merle must have had a busier day than usual because the little guy was in full nap-mode in his blanket. Dolly wasn't home. You would think I'd worry about my animals wandering free at night, but there was never a time when they weren't back by morning. I hoped that would always be the case.

Merle and Dolly share a water bottle, just like the type you'd find in a pet rabbit cage. I removed the bottle, noticed it was only half-full, and took it into the kitchen and filled it up. I made it halfway back to the cage when a van pulled up. Unwavering, I returned the water bottle to its place, and as I finished the task I saw Laurel, Fran, Steve, and Russell get off the bus and into the van. I waved as the van pulled away and left the park.

Once the van disappeared from the lot, I walked over to the bus and tried to open the door. The door was locked up tight, which I expected. Undeterred, I walked to the back wheels of the bus, then crawled underneath and rolled over onto my back. A third of the way under, I found the panel that Tommy had described.

I had brought no tools with me, but it turns out I didn't need any. There were two latches that reminded me of the ones on airplane doors, and I turned them to unlock, and the panel dropped open.

If ever there was a time when I was happy I was as small as I am, it was now. I sat up and put my arms into the hole, then easily stood. The floor level of the bus was above my waist, but not by much, so I could get into Toby's room with no trouble at all.

Now that I was inside, I went directly to Russell's room. There, I emptied the drawer and opened the false panel. The top document was the life insurance policy for Toby. I lifted it out and placed it face-down on the floor. To my surprise, the next three documents were also life insurance policies for Fran, Gabe, and Laurel. All were worth five-hundred thousand dollars, and each had the double indemnity clause for wrongful death. The beneficiary for each was the same trust listed in Toby's policy.

Just beneath the insurance policy documents were a pile of papers related to the business. They included boring things like expense reports and tax documents. I stood up and looked at the bookshelf beyond Russell's desk. There were several binders, two of which were labeled expense reports and tax documents. I grabbed the two binders, brought them back to the dresser, and sat back down on the floor. There, I compared the expense reports first, and although it took me a little while to figure out how to read the things, I determined that there were two reports. The official one in the binder had numbers that were thousands of dollars higher than the one in the drawer. I compared them, month after month, and the results were all the same. The expense reports were off.

Next, I checked the tax forms, and there were discrepancies in those as well. They had prepared the taxes in the binders in such a way to lessen the tax burden, or to ensure the largest refund possible. It proved to me that Russell was indeed playing fast and extremely loose with the accounts.

I saw everything I needed to see for now, so I returned everything to its rightful place, then went over and looked at Russell's closest. It wasn't a large closet, only about three feet wide, and I opened the door and peered inside. On the closet floor were six pairs of shoes. I removed the shoes, then rapped on the floorboard. It felt hollow for me. At the rear right corner, there was a small notch, and I put my index finger in there and popped out the floor.

"Holy cow," I said.

Beneath the floor were at least fifty pill bottles. I lifted one and saw it held the same label as the one Laurel had found in Gabe's room. Dozens of bags of pills took up the rest of the space. Most of them were gallon sized, but there were several each of quart, sandwich, and snack sized bags as well. The small ones I found were half the size of a credit card and contained only two pills each.

Although we'd only found two pills in Gabe's things, there were at least a dozen other colored tablets in Russell's stash. I pulled out a final baggie, and that one contained empty capsules. Capsules that matched Gabe's poisoned pills.

I had all the answers and proof that I needed to finger Russell for several crimes. Now what I needed to do was put everything back the way I found it and call out the calvary. I started by replacing the floorboard and putting back Russell's shoes where I found them.

Once I looked around to make sure everything was as it was before I arrived, I left the room and closed the door behind me. I was about to head for the door, but then I saw the shine of headlights pierce the windshield.

"Oh, no. They're back early."

I ducked back into the shadows until the light passed, then

quickly made my way back to Toby's room. Plan A was to go out the main door, and lock it behind me, then go back and close the hatch, but I had to put Plan B into action instead. I rushed to Toby's room and closed the door behind me.

I heard voices as I sat on the floor and swung my legs into the hatch. The voices were getting louder, and I dropped through the floor and onto the hard ground below. I let out a small yelp as my knees hit the concrete, and I prayed it wasn't loud enough for anyone to hear.

Hinges connected the hatch on one side, so all I needed to do was swing it up and close the latches to lock it. I secured the final latch just in time to hear footsteps above my head. Frozen, I waited until it was silent above me, then I crawled the length of the bus. I waited near the front right tire, and when I thought the coast was clear, I rolled out from beneath the bus, then trotted over to mine.

By the time I got back, I was panting from the stress. I found the water I'd started earlier, then drained the bottle. My right knee hurt, so I pulled down my jeans and saw something had pierced through the fabric and cut my knee. It was bleeding. I grabbed the first aid kit, rinsed the blood away with some hydrogen peroxide, then determined all it needed was a strip of cloth first aid tape to cover it.

Once I had myself back together, it was time to put in a call to Sheriff Cross.

CHAPTER THIRTEEN

Once I got my pulse below that of a hummingbird's, I called the sheriff's station and asked to be put directly in contact with Sheriff Cross. In the movies and television shows I've seen, it was a matter of whoever simply transferring the call, but in real life, it was no easy feat. I had to explain myself and stress the importance of my call to the dispatcher and two deputies before the second deputy took my phone number and told me to sit tight.

Twenty minutes later, my phone played *On the Road Again,* so at last I got a call back.

"Hello?"

"Is this Codi?"

"Yes. Is this Sheriff Cross?"

"Make it quick, Codi. I'm at an accident scene here. What's so important?"

"I've got more evidence for you on the Toby Madden murder."

I caught a huff of exasperation over the line. "What is it this time? A soup spoon?"

"Don't be condescending. I found papers that prove that Toby's manager is embezzling money and selling drugs. He also has life insurance policies for not only Toby, but for everyone else in the band."

"So what? Lots of people have life insurance."

"Yeah, but most don't have policies that pay out for four million bucks."

"Okay, okay, I'll come over after I'm done at this scene."

"No, it can't wait. They'll be leaving soon, driving right on out of here, and you'll never get them."

"Hold on."

I could tell the sheriff took the phone from his ear, and I could hear him in the background barking out orders to other people.

"Okay. I'll be there in ten minutes."

He disconnected the call without saying goodbye. Afterward, I played the waiting game again. I started pacing, wearing a hole in the floor, like my mother used to say. To pass the time and dispel some of my nervous energy, I tracked down Gibson and gave him a cat treat. He wasn't happy I woke him from what appeared to be a delightful dream based on his tail twitches, but he appreciated the salmon-flavored treat I fed him. He started out defiant, but I got a fair share of purrs in the end.

I saw red and blue flashing lights approaching, so I set Gibson back where I found him and rushed outside. By the time I got there, the sheriff had parked and stepped from his truck.

"Okay, tell me what you got."

I was about to spill the complete story, but I stopped before I began. The problem slapped me right in the head. I slipped up. I had found Russell's dirt while in the process of committing a crime myself. The sheriff would consider it either trespassing or breaking and entering, and I imagined that would taint the evidence I gathered. I realized too late I should have called the lawyer before I called the sheriff.

"Well? I'm waiting," he said as he glared at me.

"Sheriff, I've come into some information about criminal activity on Toby's bus. I think Russell killed Toby for insurance money, and deliberately poisoned Gabe for the same. And I also believe Russell is a drug dealer."

"Sure. Anything else?" He seemed unimpressed.

"Um, potentially tax fraud and embezzlement," I said.

I saw the sheriff roll his eyes.

"Come on, Sheriff, I'm not kidding here," I said as I crossed my arms.

"How did you come about all this information?" he asked.

I looked out into the twilight night. "I can't tell you yet."

"Do you know if anyone appears hurt or in any physical danger over there?" he asked.

I didn't know how to answer that one, but I suspected not.

"I don't think so," I admitted.

"Okay. Wait here."

I planted my feet and watched as the sheriff walked to the bus. Instead of going directly to the door, he stopped at every window, looked in, and moved on to the next window. Once he'd made a complete loop around the vehicle, he approached the door. I closed the distance to about half so I could overhear what was going on while he knocked.

Russell opened the door and stepped from the bus.

"Sheriff Cross. What a surprise. What can I do for you?"

"Mr. Davidson, we've received a tip that someone has committed one or more crimes on this bus. Do you mind if I come aboard and check it out?"

I got a sense of vindication. It was almost over. Surely, the sheriff would uncover everything I did.

Russell and Sheriff Cross got into a staring contest, and Russell broke first. "Actually, we're getting ready to leave, so no. You may not come aboard."

"Mr. Davidson, if you cooperate, I'm sure we can clear

everything up quickly and have you on your way in no time. I'm sure it won't take me more than five minutes of your time."

The sheriff stepped toward the stairs, but Russell was already there and got on the bottom step to block the way.

"Sheriff, I said no. I saw you walk around the bus, and I bet you have neither reasonable suspicion nor probable cause of any crime here. So, again, I ask you to step away and either produce a warrant to enter or let us be on our way."

Sheriff Cross stood still for a moment and tipped his hat at Russell. "Have a pleasant night, sir. Travel safe."

He turned and walked back in my direction. My internal anger thermometer was on the rise. "That's it? Have a pleasant night? You're going to let him get away?"

"Listen, there's nothing I can do right now. He's right. I can't get on the bus without an invitation or a warrant. If there is evidence of a crime and I break in to get it, anything I find wouldn't be admissible in court."

In my heart, I accepted that, because my dad had often said the same. "Based on what I told you, will you get a warrant?"

"I can try. I'll use the evidence that you found earlier to convince the judge to give me one."

"How long will that take?"

"Oh, I don't know. A couple of hours. Perhaps more."

"What about drug dogs? Bring those in. I'm sure they'd hit on something."

"We're too small a county to have our own dogs. We'd have to call them in from L.A., and that would take at least six hours before they got here."

"And what if they just drive away before that happens?"

Sheriff Cross looked at me, then at Toby's bus, then did a circle and looked around the park. He shot me a sly smile.

"I wouldn't worry about that. I'm going to go. You have a good night now."

To my surprise, the sheriff climbed into his truck, and I

watched as he drove away. When he got to the park entrance, his taillights brightened, and I could tell he'd put the truck in park. He got out, walked a circle around the truck, then got back in and drove off.

I'd felt good before, but now I seemed deflated like a five-day-old birthday balloon.

I moved inside and got a jacket to protect myself from the chilly evening, then returned outside and sat in my chair. If I couldn't get the sheriff to investigate, I thought I'd get lucky and spot Russell dragging away a body. Hopefully not Laurel's.

An hour later, the engine on Toby's bus roared to life, and I knew it was over. I looked toward them and saw Steve in the driver's seat. The headlights came on, and the bus made a small lurch as Steve shifted it into Drive. He got about ten feet when the flashing lights of a police vehicle approached and stopped directly in front of Toby's bus. It lurched again as Steve slammed on the brakes and shifted back into Park.

This time, Deputy Marvin made an appearance and glanced over at me before he headed to Toby's door. Russell was down and off the bus before Deputy Marvin got within five feet.

"This is outrageous! What do you want?" Russell screamed.

"I'm sorry, sir, you can't leave."

"Why? Do you have a warrant?"

"No, sir, there's been an accident," Deputy Marvin said.

"Accident? Where?"

"At the park entrance. A drunk driver ran into the culvert just outside the entrance. Sorry, road's blocked until the investigation is over and we can get a tow truck in here to remove the vehicle."

"I don't believe you," Russell said.

"Whether you believe me doesn't change the facts, sir. You're welcome to walk down there and take a gander for yourself."

Russell did just that. As he stomped past me, I saw his

furrowed brow and angry face. When he walked by, he huffed with every step, like an old steam-powered train engine trying to pick up speed. It was a bit of a walk to the park's entrance, and I waited for Russell to come back. Deputy Marvin stayed still where he was.

Minutes passed, and eventually Russell came huffing by on his return trip. His mood hadn't improved while he was away, and he seemed to be even angrier.

"How did you get in here?" he asked.

Deputy Marvin refocused his attention on Russell. "Well, sir, there was a deputy chasing the car headed southbound, and I was driving northbound. The alleged drunk driver attempted to play a game of chicken with me. I swerved into the park at the last second, and he drove right into the ditch."

It seemed like a logical explanation to me. Believable, almost. Russell didn't like it, though. He looked frustrated and threw his hands in the air.

"Well then. I guess we're just stuck here."

Russell got back on the bus and slammed the door in the deputy's face.

Deputy Marvin turned his attention to me next. "Ma'am, will you be okay?"

I smiled. "Sure. I'm good. I wasn't planning to go anywhere. It must have been quite the car chase with the crash and all."

Deputy Marvin shot me a sly smile. "Yes, it sure was."

"Any idea when it will get cleaned up?"

The deputy removed his hat and scratched his head. "If I had to guess, I'd say they won't have it cleaned up until mid-morning."

"I guess I'll head off to bed, then. What are you going to do, Deputy?"

"I'll be back down at the crash site to monitor things. I'll be around if you need me."

"Thank you, sir."

Deputy Marvin nodded at me, then drove away. I returned to my bus, collapsed into a chair, and when I did, I realized how tired I was. It had been a long, emotionally draining day. My body cried out for sleep, and I hoped I'd actually get some.

I passed through the bus and turned out all the lights and shut all the shades before I robotically went through my nighttime routine and slipped into my bed. I laid there on my back, staring at the dark ceiling, and listening to the quiet. It was too quiet for my taste, with not even a peep from an insect or frog to break the silence. I exhaled, knowing it was going to be a long, sleepless night.

I opened my eyes. I must have been more tired than I thought. I'd slept through the night without moving, and didn't even notice that at some point, Gibson had joined me. He was lying on my chest and was staring at me with his pretty green eyes.

"Good morning. Did you sleep well? Can I get up?"

Gibson licked my nose once, then stood, stretched, and jumped from the bed. I threw back the covers, put my feet on the floor, and looked at my phone. It was just after six-thirty in the morning, and it was time to rise.

After I visited the bathroom and brushed my teeth, I fed Gibson, then checked the fridge for something to feed Merle and Dolly. I knew they probably spent the night dining on whatever they could scavenge, but I still liked to give them their daily bread. Since I was running low on fruits and vegetables, I pulled a tofu-based hot dog from the freezer, cut it in half, and put it with the lettuce and carrots I had.

I reminded myself again that I needed to go out for groceries, and if I didn't do it soon, I'd have to rely on eating whatever Dolly and Merle could bring back for me.

I changed out of my pajama bottoms and into my jeans, then rather than attend to my hair, I put on a baseball cap. Finally ready to face the world, I unlocked the door and stepped outside.

I half-expected Toby's bus to be gone, but it was right where Steve had parked the beast the night before. Deputy Marvin wasn't in sight, but I had a feeling he was around somewhere.

I checked on Merle and Dolly, who were both in for the day. Merle was napping, and Dolly was playing with a shiny rock she'd found somewhere. She was always bringing home treasures, and after I dropped the food into their bowls, I checked underneath her blanket to look for her secret stash. In it, she had another rock and an orange golf ball. I didn't feel the need to confiscate any of her booty, so I replaced the blanket, gave them both head scratches, and closed the door. If there was going to be trouble this morning, I didn't want my pets in the middle of it.

Next, I went to check on Tommy. I stepped around the bus, fully expecting to see him asleep on the chair, but I was wrong. Tommy was gone. He had been there. The blanket, which I had spread out for him the night before, appeared neatly folded, and one of the water bottles was empty. I wondered where he could be, either in the woods, or in the shower house, but in the end, it was his business, so I put him from my mind.

My stomach growled, so I got back on the bus to feed myself. I found a quarter-loaf of bread and was in the middle of preparing a gourmet peanut butter and jelly sandwich when I saw the sheriff's truck pull up and park. From the window, I watched as he got out of the truck, papers in hand, and walked over to Toby's bus.

He knocked on the door, and Steve answered. Steve took the paper, read it, and let the sheriff in. I finished making the sandwich, cut it in half, put it on a plate, and took it outside. It was a glorious morning for breakfast outdoors.

Deputy Marvin pulled up and nodded at me when he got out of his truck, then waited outside the bus. A few minutes later, Steve emerged, followed by Russell. Russell wasn't saying anything, but the way he displayed his body language told me he was angry about the early morning intrusion.

Next off the bus stepped Fran. She was dressed in a dark blue nightgown. Satin, I guessed, based on the way it reflected the morning sunlight. She also wore a long black robe but didn't bother to close it. Laurel was the last passenger to exit the bus. She was more modestly dressed in gray sweatpants and a plain charcoal-colored T-shirt. Laurel spotted me and came my way. She plopped down into Bozeman's chair.

"Good morning," she said.

I held out the plate, offering her the sandwich half I hadn't touched yet. "Morning. Peanut butter and jelly sandwich?"

"Sure." Laurel accepted the sandwich and took a bite. She chewed for a bit, and then swallowed it down. "That's good. I can't remember the last time I had a peanut butter sandwich."

I smiled. "We eat them all the time. What's going on over there?"

"For some strange reason, the sheriff showed up this morning with a warrant to check over the bus. Something about drugs. I didn't get all the details. I was just told to get off the bus while he conducted the search."

"Do you think he'll find what we need him to?" I asked.

Laurel winked at me. "Well, I may have accidentally let it slip that there are several secret compartments within the furniture and closets on board. He just smiled at me and asked me to leave the bus."

"Interesting. I hope he finds what he's looking for."

"Me, too," Laurel said.

Laurel and I ate our sandwiches and watched the activity near the other bus. Russell and Steve stood nearby the bus and waited. Fran had an animated conversation with Deputy Marvin about something. Finally, Fran took off her robe and spun in a circle. The deputy nodded. Fran replaced her robe, then took off for the shower house.

"What do you think that was about?"

"We're all supposed to stay within view of the good deputy.

They want to make sure we smuggled nothing off the bus or that we get into any other trouble."

"I didn't see him try to stop you. Why was that?"

"Oh, the sheriff himself checked me over before I left the bus, so I got his blessing. Besides, the deputy can see me from there, so I'm good."

It took about an hour before Sheriff Cross emerged from the bus. Once he did, he waved me over.

Laurel seemed concerned by the gesture. "Uh, oh. What's that about?"

"I don't know. Wait here, and I'll go find out."

I walked over to the bus and gestured for me to join him onboard.

Before I could get my foot on the first step, Russell objected. "Hey, what's going on? Where's she going?"

The sheriff didn't even acknowledge him, but Deputy Marvin stepped in front of Russell to impede him from going any further. "Police business, sir. Please step back and relax."

Sheriff Cross came up behind me. "Go. Keep moving."

Once we were both aboard, I turned around. "What's going on?"

Cross moved ahead of me. "Ms. Preston let slip about potential hiding spots in here. Come with me."

Our first stop was Gabe's room. Someone had removed the panel. Gabe's nude magazine was still there, but there was nothing else in the drawer.

"So?" I asked.

"So porn isn't illegal in this state. There's nothing here," the sheriff said.

We passed Fran's room, and the sheriff pointed to it as we passed. "Nothing of interest in there."

The next stop was Toby's room. I could tell Cross had done a thorough search in there, as everything looked out of order. He guided me to the closet, and I looked in. He'd found the panel, but there was nothing beneath it.

"See? It's empty."

We left and walked right by Laurel's hovel without comment. I knew from being in there before there were no secrets, other than her classical music training and unorthodox violin.

To his credit, Cross had gone through Russell's room with a fine-toothed comb. He'd removed all the books from the shelves, all the dresser drawers were empty, the desk looked rummaged through, and the closet was open.

He led me to the dresser first. "Come over here and look."

I looked at the bottom drawer. He'd removed the false bottom, but the contents looked different. I bent over, went through the drawer, and found it filled with random things related to Toby. There were promotional flyers, old set lists, articles clipped from newspapers, and what looked to be fan mail.

"What? No, this isn't right!" I said.

I got up and rushed to the closet. The false bottom was leaning against the closet door. I looked in and saw several shoe boxes. I opened the lid of the first box and found a new pair of golf cleats. The second box contained the whitest pair of Converse I'd ever seen. I flipped open the covers of the other four pairs and found the same thing in each box. Shoes.

I picked up a sneaker, looked at it, and threw it back down. I felt frustrated and flustered. All the evidence that pointed to Russell's crimes was gone. "No, this isn't right. Drugs filled up this whole thing. And in the dresser were the insurance policies."

The sheriff leaned on the doorjamb and crossed his arms. "You want to explain to me how you knew that?"

"Because I…" My brain finally caught up with my tongue, so I stopped speaking. The last thing I needed was to be arrested. "Because I had it on good authority, that's how."

He dropped his arms and shook his head. "Look, I'm sorry. I found nothing. Not so much as an unpaid parking ticket shoved into the glove compartment."

"Wait. I'll bet if you brought in the dogs, they'd hit on something. They'd bust this case wide open."

"Codi, I know you're trying to help your friend out of a jam, but trying to get someone else in trouble isn't the way to do it. I'm sorry, but I found no evidence of any crime. Come on, let's go."

I didn't like to whine, but I started to and pleaded with him. "But wait, you're making a mistake!"

"No. Stop. You're wrong. I repeat, for the last time. There. Is. Zero. I. Can. Do. There's no evidence. I'm a cop, I work from evidence, and the only evidence I have points to Jesse James as a murderer."

Dejected, I turned and left Russell's room. I walked directly down the stairs, over to my bus, and entered my home without saying a word to anyone. That included Laurel, who wore a confused look as I passed by without comment. I sunk into a chair and put my head in my hands. I had failed. Failed myself, and failed Bozeman.

I heard a light knock at the door, but I didn't bother to get up and answer it.

"Go away."

I said the words so silently that I was the only one who could have heard them.

The knock repeated, and I said the words again, this time louder. I heard the door open, and a few seconds later, Laurel was by my side. She said nothing, but leaned over and gave me a warm hug.

"It's all gone. All the evidence I found. Cleared out. Gone, and there's nothing we can do about it," I said.

Laurel held the hug to comfort me, which I appreciated. Then, suddenly, she let go and pushed away.

"Hey, Codi? Why is Tommy outside your window waving at us like a madman?"

CHAPTER FOURTEEN

I looked out the window to where Laurel was pointing and indeed Tommy was outside, trying to get my attention.

"Stay here," I said.

"Are you going to be okay? I can come with you." Laurel asked.

"Of course. I'll be fine. He's harmless. Besides, I've got a gun."

I did a double check and made sure Betty was with me, then I stepped off the bus and around the back. Tommy was waiting for me, moving his weight from one leg to another like he was a toddler needing to use the bathroom.

"What's your deal?" I asked.

"What's going on? Are they here for me?" Tommy asked, looking around him as he spoke.

"No. They're not here for you. Why would they be? For a vagrancy charge?"

I heard a couple of doors slam, so I walked around the bus. The lawmen were driving away. Steve and Russell were nowhere in sight, so I guessed they'd returned to their bus. I returned to

Tommy.

"The cops are gone. You've got nothing to worry about."

"But why were they even here?" he asked, still frightened.

I gave him a loud, extended exhale. "They were here because they were looking for drugs and other stuff. Yesterday I used that panel you told me about and broke into the bus. I found a whole stash of drugs and a bunch of paperwork that proves Russell is up to his eyebrows in questionable things, so I called the sheriff. He executed a search warrant this morning, but he came up empty. Everything I found yesterday afternoon was gone by this morning."

I looked at Tommy and he had an expression on his face that I didn't quite place. "What? Are you shocked I did what I did?"

Tommy shook it off. "No. It's not that. I watched them last night."

"Watched who?"

"I couldn't really tell who it was in the dark. They slipped off into the woods. They were gone for maybe twenty minutes and came back."

"You think you could show me where they went?" I asked.

Tommy thought for a moment. "I guess so."

"Okay, lead the way. I don't want to be seen by anyone, so let's stay out of view."

Tommy nodded and started off into the nearest clump of trees. I followed Tommy, and before long, we arrived at his makeshift camp. On a tree stump sat an open can of baked beans with a spoon sticking out of it.

"Last night I saw the weirdest thing. I was sitting right there on that stump having a snack when a raccoon walked right past me carrying a golf ball. It was orange. Can you imagine that?"

I chuckled. "Nope. Not in a million years. Where to next?"

Tommy led me along the deer trail I'd followed the previous day, and eventually we came to the junction I'd found. There, he stopped and looked around. I remembered the left path headed to the parking lot.

"Well, should we go straight ahead, or turn right? Which way?"

"Let's try right," he said.

I followed Tommy down the right trail. It started out about eight inches wide, but after a hundred yards, it narrowed down to nothing. The trail ended at a bramble of shrubs with long thorns I couldn't identify.

We turned around, found the junction, and took a right turn. We followed the trail for perhaps a quarter mile and the area opened up to a spot that contained several downed trees.

"Hey, Tommy, do you think whoever you saw was carrying anything?"

"Possibly, sure," he said.

"Okay. Let's spread out here and check around all these trees for anything they may have hidden, okay?"

"Like what?" he asked.

"Beats me. A garbage bag? A box? Perhaps a plastic tote? Who knows what they would have hidden? Look around, okay?"

We separated. I headed into the trees from where we were, while Tommy walked farther down the trail to examine another group of trees. I made my way through and checked both sides of every downed tree, and behind each one in the vicinity still standing. Several minutes of searching brought me no results, except a disturbed squirrel who chittered at me as I passed him.

I was about to give up and move on to a new location when Tommy whistled. I looked around and spotted him thirty yards away. Rather than pick my way through the trees, I backtracked to the deer path and headed in his direction from there. When I was fifteen feet from him, I saw the largest downed tree in the area complete with an exposed root ball.

"Back here. Go around to the left. The right is kind of thorny."

I took Tommy's directions, and soon I was next to him.

Obscured by the roots and stacked branches were two small suitcases.

Tommy moved the branches and reached for the suitcase handle.

On impulse, I reached out and slapped his hand. The retort echoed in the trees. "Sorry about that. Don't touch the handle. In case there are fingerprints."

Tommy nodded. "Yeah, good idea."

Tommy reached again, this time for one of the suitcases' roller wheels. He grabbed the wheel, gave a tug, and dislodged the case. The suitcase was about the size of a small carry-on and looked zippered shut.

"Hold on." Slowly, I made my way to the other side of the tree, where there were indeed ground vines with thorns. I found a section where the vine was thin, and doing my best to avoid the prickers, broke the vine away in a section about five inches long. I returned to Tommy and fed the vine through the zipper's hole and looped it. Pulling on the vine, I moved the zipper and opened the case.

Tommy seemed impressed. "That's a smart move!"

After I unzipped the case, I used a stick to open it. I looked in and discovered it stuffed with paperwork, and right on top was the insurance policy on Fran.

"This is good. Pull out the other one."

As I closed the suitcase and zipped it up, Tommy struggled to get the other case.

"Heavy?"

Tommy nodded. "Yeah. Probably twice the weight."

That seemed logical, since the second suitcase was about twice the size of the previous one. Again, I applied the vine trick and unzipped and opened it.

"Oh, wow," Tommy said.

"Yeah, for sure," I answered.

The second case held all the drugs. The ones in plastic

baggies sat on top, but I used the stick to move those aside and uncovered all the mislabeled vitamin bottles.

"Bingo," I said.

"Now what? Should we put them back?" Tommy asked.

I thought about it for a moment and decided against it. "No. I think that's a bad idea. Why don't we take them back to your camp? Can you handle that?"

"I think so."

"Can you carry the bigger one?"

Tommy nodded. "Sure. No problem. No handles, right?"

"Right." Since I was closest to the trail, I turned the smaller suitcase upside-down and lifted it by the wheels. I struggled to get it through the underbrush, but eventually I made it to the trail. There I stopped and looked for Tommy, but he was right behind me.

I took the lead and trudged on, struggling with the case as I walked. I plodded on for another ten yards when I received a quiet whistle from behind me. When I looked behind, Tommy had stopped. The suitcase was on the ground, and he was leaning against a tree, breathing hard. I put my case down and stepped back to him.

"Sorry. It's so heavy. I don't think I can do this," he said, his breathing turning to wheezing.

"Okay. Wait here. I'll be right back."

I returned to the smaller case, picked it up, and started walking as fast as I could manage while carrying the awkward load. After a couple of minutes, I passed the trail junction. Five minutes later, I spotted the pillowcases, and the bean can. I set the suitcase down and trotted down the trail back to Tommy. He didn't look well. He was still breathing hard and looked pale.

"I'll help you carry this one, okay?"

He nodded.

"If you can't do it, let me know, and I can find another way. I have a hand truck on the bus, but I'd probably attract attention getting it out, so I'd rather we carry it, okay?"

He nodded again. "You've given me enough rest. I can go on."

"Great. I'll lift the wheels and walk backwards. You grip it by the sides. Remember, don't touch the handle."

"Got it. You can count on me."

We bent over together, and I grabbed the wheels and lifted. Tommy picked up the other end. He couldn't get a good grip, so he rested the suitcase on his forearms. Slowly, we started moving.

"Tell me if I'm going to ram into a tree or something," I said.

"Sure. You're going good. Keep it slow, and we'll be fine."

We moved at a turtle's pace along the trail since I needed to check every footstep so I wouldn't trip over anything. The suitcase was too heavy for me, even with the help of another person, but I didn't want to drop it and give up. After fifteen minutes of struggling, we finally reached Tommy's camp, and we set the case down.

Tommy brushed the bean can from the tree stump and sat down.

"Are you okay?" I asked.

"I'm fine. I need a rest and to catch my breath. Give me a couple of minutes and I'll be okay."

"Can you watch this stuff while I get the sheriff back here?"

Tommy nodded. I could tell he was tired, and I hoped he wouldn't doze off while I was gone. I hated to leave him that way, but I didn't have a choice.

From the campsite, I rushed back to my bus. As I turned the corner, I found Laurel out in the parking lot having an argument with Russell.

"You can't just leave us here!" Laurel yelled.

"So, get out of the way!" Russell screamed back.

I saw the bus inch forward. Steve was behind the wheel. I could tell he was looking at Laurel, who was certainly in the way, and I feared he would hit the gas and run her down.

I jumped onto my bus and checked my pockets for the keys. They weren't in there. I didn't have the time to search all over the bus for where I had left them last, so I ran directly to Bozeman's room. There, on the desk next to his wallet, were his keys. I grabbed them and rushed to the driver's seat.

"Oh, man," I said.

I looked out and saw Toby's bus inch closer to Laurel. While I appreciated her bravery, I questioned her sanity.

I shoved the key into the ignition and started the bus. Bozeman was the designated bus driver, so the way he positioned the seat was farther back than I could work with. I positioned my butt on the front edge of the driver's seat and pressed the brake pedal. Satisfied I was as ready as I was going to get, I put the bus in reverse and cranked the steering wheel all the way to the left.

I took my foot off the brake, and the bus swung backward. I laid on the horn to get Laurel's attention. She looked behind her and I saw the fear in her eyes when she realized she was in danger of getting sandwiched between sixty thousand pounds of steel.

Laurel made a quick decision and ran out of the way.

I saw Toby's bus speed up, and I tapped the gas to increase my momentum. The bus swung wildly around and before I knew it; there I was facing the woods instead of the other bus.

I felt a slight nudge when the buses kissed each other, and I put mine into Park and turned off the engine. I rushed to the door, opened it, and locked eyes with Steve, who was only a foot and a windshield away from me. With my hand, I motioned to him to back up his bus. He reversed it about four feet and parked.

From my bus, I ran directly to theirs and started my fake outrage the moment the door opened.

"You idiot! Steve, you hit me! You could have killed me! I'm calling the police."

Russell appeared, to his credit, equally antagonistic. "Screw you, Codi. You got in our way. We're leaving."

"Go ahead. Then the cops can arrest you for fleeing the scene of an accident, too."

Russell dismissed me with a wave. "Steve, let's go."

I'd had enough of the game. I pulled Betty from the holster, stepped in front of the door, and took a shooter's stance. "Steve. Turn off the bus."

Steve took one look at my gun and switched off the vehicle.

"Good boy. Now toss the keys down here."

Steve complied, and Laurel scampered over and picked them up.

"Now, both of you. Get off the bus."

Russell and Steve got off the bus with their hands in the air. Honestly, for an impromptu plan, the results pleased me so far, even though I was in the middle of committing a felony myself.

"Laurel, would you mind calling the sheriff for me?"

Laurel did as I asked and placed the call. As she finished up, Fran made an appearance from the shower house.

"What did I miss?"

Laurel chuckled. "Quite a lot, actually. The cops will be here momentarily."

Everyone stood where they were and waited. Off in the distance, I heard the peal of the siren, and soon after, the sheriff and two of his deputies rolled into the lot. As soon as Sheriff Cross stepped out of his truck, I placed my gun on the ground and put my hands in the air.

Before I could count to ten, I was face down on the pavement and I felt the cold steel of handcuffs on my wrists. It was an odd sensation, one I've never had before, and one I wanted to avoid in the future.

Sheriff Cross picked up my gun, removed the clip, and put it on his truck's hood. He lifted me to my feet.

"What's going on here now?" he asked.

Russell stepped forward first. "That nutty woman pulled a

gun on us. I want her arrested for assault and unlawful restraint."

Cross turned to me. "Is this true?"

"Partially. Steve, the driver over there, tried to run over Laurel and hit my bus. And then, when I told him to stop, Russell ordered him to drive away. That's felony hit and run. I was justified in keeping him at the scene."

Sheriff Cross literally growled. "I'm so glad I have so many lawyers here. Boys, cuff these other two until we can figure this out."

The deputies moved with haste, and within two minutes, Russell and Steve had bracelets that looked just like mine.

The sheriff turned to Steve. "You have anything to say?"

Steve glanced at Russell, then shook his head. "No comment."

Cross spun around and addressed Laurel. "What about you?"

Laurel looked at him straight on. "It's just like Codi said. They were trying to leave without us, and I stepped in front of the bus to stop them, but they kept coming at me. Then Codi pulled her bus out, and Steve hit her, then Russell wanted him to just drive away."

"Who's us?" Sheriff Cross asked.

"What?"

"You said they were trying to leave without us."

"Oh. Me and Fran," Laurel said.

Fran was up next for questioning.

"What do you have to add?" the sheriff asked.

Fran smiled. "Actually, nothing. I was in the bathroom. I just got back here when you did, so I didn't see or hear anything."

"How convenient for you," Sheriff Cross said.

"Hey, am I interrupting anything?"

I looked over and saw Tommy holding the smaller suitcase by the wheels. I turned just in time to see the look that Russell and Steve passed between each other.

"Who are you?"

I stepped over. "Sheriff, that's Tommy Skye. Within that suitcase is all the documentation you were looking for yesterday."

Fran walked toward Tommy. "Hey, what are you doing with my suitcase? I was looking for that."

"Hold it there, ma'am," Deputy Marvin said. Fran stopped in her tracks.

"Bring that over here, Lee."

Deputy Marvin took the case from Tommy, set it on the ground next to the sheriff's truck, and opened it up. The sheriff looked inside, then grabbed a corner of the top document, removed it from the case, and glanced at the document below it.

"I've seen enough. Anyone want to explain these?"

No one said a word, then Tommy spoke up. "I've got another case, but I can't carry it myself. Can I take your deputy with me to get it?"

"You lead the way and keep your hands in sight, okay?"

Tommy walked off, followed by Deputy Marvin, and within three minutes, they were back. Deputy Marvin set the suitcase next to the first one and unzipped it. All three officers looked in disbelief at the drug-stuffed case.

A movement caught my eye. "Hey. Officer. Someone's making a break for it."

Sheriff Cross looked up from the case and saw Steve making a break for the woods. "Deputy, please bring that idiot back."

Deputy Marvin took off running. I heard him shout a couple of times, and then all was silent. Moments later, the deputy returned, walking with Steve ahead of him. Marvin's shirt was untucked, and Steve had a bloody nose.

"What happened?" Sheriff Cross asked.

"He resisted arrest, Sheriff. I had to tackle him."

"Why don't you put him in the back of your truck? Obviously, he's under arrest."

Deputy Marvin did as ordered, then rejoined the group.

"Do you have anything you want to say yet?" Sheriff Cross asked Russell.

Russell was getting nervous. "It was all him, Sheriff. He's a drug dealer. He's got contacts and makes sales all over the west coast."

"You're saying when I run fingerprints over all those drugs, I won't find yours anywhere?"

"No. Yes. Yes, you will, but he made me do it. Please understand. He's been threatening me my entire life. That guy is pure evil. He would have killed me if I didn't help him."

"Your entire life?"

"Yes, Sheriff. Steve's my cousin. He forced me to be a mule for him."

"Okay, fine. Now, what about all these documents? These life insurance policies? Are you involved in any of that?"

Russell had enough of answering questions and clammed up. I didn't blame him. It was actually a good idea to pin the drug stuff on his cousin. Dealing drugs was a lot worse than whatever white-collar nonsense Russell was involved in.

"I guess that's it then. Put him in my car," the sheriff said.

"Wait! There's something else. I'll be right back." Laurel ran onto the bus and returned with a laptop. She put it on the hood next to my gun and adjusted the screen so everyone could see it. She opened a video file and Fran's image came on the screen.

"You don't get it. I can destroy your career. It will all be over. Everyone in music will find out about your lack of talent and desire to sleep your way to the top."

I'd only talked to Toby a few times, but the disembodied voice on the video was his.

On the video, Fran smiled. "Oh sweetie, tell whoever you want. I don't really care, but I'm sure your wife will when it all comes out."

The video suddenly ended. "Sorry. I opened the wrong file.

Let's try this one."

Laurel clicked on another file and let it play. The camera was in the same position, but it was Russell's face on the screen. It took a couple of seconds, but Toby's voice came through the speakers.

"Game's up, Russell. I know all about your cousin and his drug running."

The on-screen Russell hesitated, then spoke. "So, what are you going to do? Call the cops?"

"No. I'm going to take a cut. I'm sure that's the easiest thing for everyone around here. He keeps making money, you keep making money, and I make money. Money, money, money. Enough to go around, and everyone's happy. "

"I'll have to talk to Steve about it. Make sure he approves."

"Oh, he'll approve. Otherwise, he must just find himself buried in a hole in the desert. Get my drift?"

"Yeah. I got it." Russell turned away, but Toby's hand came into the frame and grabbed Russell's shoulder. "Wait. I'm not done with you yet."

"What?" Russell's tone was snarky.

"I also discovered that you've been playing with the numbers. Oh, you're good at it, but you almost got caught. An accountant from the record company called looking for you and asked about one of the expense reports. You were out somewhere that day, so I told her I'd look into it. She sent me a copy over the phone, and lo-and-behold, I stumbled across your secret stash."

"What's your point?"

"The point is, I want in on that too, or you'll be on your way to prison. And if you go, Steve goes. You're doing all the hard work, so I'll make it easy on you. Fifty-one, forty-nine split, and you get the higher percentage."

Russell looked dead on at the camera, so I assumed Toby had it positioned somewhere above and to the left of where Toby was sitting.

"Listen, you no-talent hack. Fine, you'll get the money, but you'd better watch your back from now on, because I know things about you, too. Like you're cheating on your wife, and I know you're cheating on your taxes. And I know you're stealing songs from other songwriters without compensating them. Remember that minor incident in Nashville? Do you think I don't know of the other dozen instances of intellectual property theft you've committed? You may think you have me over a barrel, but we're over the same barrel. We're done here."

The video played for a few more seconds, then faded to black.

"Who was the man not on camera?" the sheriff asked.

Laurel spoke up. "The murder victim. Toby Madden. That's his voice."

Sheriff Cross closed the laptop. "I have to take this into evidence, too."

"That's fine. It belonged to Toby. He won't need it," Laurel said.

The two deputies transferred all the evidence into the third deputy's car. While they did, Sheriff Cross turned me around and unlocked my handcuffs. Then he handed Betty and the clip to me.

"You know, it was a nice bluff. They could have taken you down, even if you had shot someone. Rubber bullets do minor damage."

I smiled. "Yeah, but they didn't know that."

CHAPTER FIFTEEN

The next morning I woke with a horrible pain in my neck.

The night before, once the police left, I invited Laurel and Fran over for a beer. Laurel accepted, but Fran didn't. I imagined the loss of her meal ticket disturbed her and she was dreading going back into the real world.

Laurel had one of Bozeman's beers, and I drank a cola, and we stayed up and talked most of the night. Bozeman's beer turned out to be too much for Laurel, and she fell asleep in her chair. I covered her up with a blanket and I sat in the other chair. My intention was to stay there for only a few minutes before I continued off to bed, but Gibson jumped in my lap and got comfortable. He purred himself to sleep, and the next thing I realized, sunlight was streaming in through the window and my neck wouldn't cooperate.

I counted to three, held my breath, and twisted my neck from side to side. There was instant pain, and I could have sworn I heard something pop, but it immediately seemed better.

I fed Gibson, and wanted to wake Laurel, but she was sleeping soundly and snoring softly, so I didn't have the heart to do so. Instead, I gathered some things and went for a long, hot shower.

When I got back to the bus, Laurel was awake and nursing a bottle of water.

"I'm sorry. I can't believe I slept so long," Laurel said.

"Hey, it's not a problem, really. You want some breakfast?"

She smiled. "Peanut butter and jelly again?"

I opened the fridge and grabbed the strawberry preserves. I opened the jar and looked inside. "Well, we're out of jelly, so it'll only be peanut butter."

Laurel crinkled her nose. "You mean by itself? What kind of psycho eats peanut butter by itself? I've got a better idea. How about some pancakes?"

It took me a fraction of a second to mull it over. "Sure. I love pancakes. Do you use real maple syrup or the fake stuff?"

"Oh, the real maple syrup. Direct from Vermont. It's the only way to go. We might be out of pecans though, so you'd have to choose between regular, blueberry, or chocolate chip pancakes." Laurel understood how to tease me.

I grinned. "I love blueberries."

"Me too. Let's go," Laurel said.

Laurel and I left my bus and stepped into hers. She led me into the kitchen, and she started gathering the ingredients for breakfast.

"Do you want sausage or bacon?" she asked.

That was a simple choice for me, too. "Bacon. The answer is always bacon, even when bacon isn't an option."

Laurel chuckled. "I get what you mean. I'm with you there. Um, I hate to do this, but can you start breakfast while I run for a quick shower? I'll be back in ten minutes, fifteen at the most."

"Yeah. Of course. I'll get things ready, and we'll save the pancakes until you get back. Oh, before you go though, do you like your bacon crispy or not so crispy?"

"I prefer it not so crispy, but I'll eat it any way it comes out."

Laurel disappeared into her space and came out a few seconds later with her backpack. As she rushed out of the door, I opened the cabinets, looking for a frying pan.

"It's the far cabinet on the right, down below."

I looked over, and Fran was standing in the hallway. She looked less like a supermodel and more like a woman who'd gone through the ringer.

"Thanks. Would you like to join us for breakfast?" I asked.

Fran shrugged. "Sure. Might as well. Do you want some coffee?"

"No. I don't drink it."

Fran laughed. "Neither does Laurel. I don't understand people who can actually wake up in the morning and be productive without coffee."

While Fran made a pot, I retrieved the largest frying pan I could, set it on the range top, and layered the bacon in the pan. By the time Fran was sipping her first cup, the smell of cooking bacon wafted through the bus.

"That smells so good." Laurel said as she returned, dropped her backpack on the floor next to the door and joined us in the kitchen. "Want some juice or some tea?"

"Juice would be good."

Laurel pulled out two glasses from the cabinet next to my head and poured glasses of orange juice for both of us. Then she grabbed a bowl and started making the pancake batter. It was an instant mix, but I didn't complain.

Fifteen minutes later, the three of us clustered around the dinette table. Laurel had opted for a short stack of chocolate chip pancakes. I went with three fresh blueberry ones, and Fran had a single plain pancake. The plate of bacon sat in the table's center, within reach of everyone.

"Now that this is over, what's next for you two?" I asked.

Unlike Laurel and me, Fran opted to eat her pancake without syrup. She also ate it without a fork. Instead, she tore pieces off with her fingers and ate it that way. She swallowed what she was chewing and took a sip from her third cup of coffee.

"I talked to a rep of the record company last night. They're sending another driver in from the city to take the bus. I imagine it'll pass on to the next up-and-coming star," Fran said.

"What about you, personally?" I asked.

Fran shrugged. "I don't have any idea. I'm kind of tired of music. The money's not as good as I imagined it would be, and I get bored easily. And I really miss the excitement of the city. I'm not worried though. I'll land on my feet somewhere."

"What about you, Laurel?" I asked.

"Like I said the other day, I'm not sure. I've been wanting to visit my grandmother, so perhaps I'll take a break and do that. After that, I'll be looking for another place to play. I love playing for people."

I nodded. "I understand that. Playing music for people is even better than bacon."

"Hey," Fran said.

Laurel and I looked at her. Fran took the last strip of bacon and held it out before her. "There's nothing better than bacon."

Laurel and I laughed as Fran ate the slice, then Laurel got up and collected the plates. I pitched in and did the dishes while Laurel cleaned the rest of the kitchen.

After we were done, I said goodbye to them both and stepped off the bus. I was halfway back to mine when I saw the sheriff's truck approaching.

"Oh, no. Now what?" I asked no one.

I stopped and waited for him to get to me. "Hey there. I brought you a present."

The sheriff stepped around to the back seat and opened the door. Bozeman stepped out wearing the biggest smile I'd ever seen on his face. He came over and gave me a bear hug that almost squeezed the life from me.

"I need a beer, and a shower, and another beer."

"But it's only ten o'clock. Bozeman!" I was too late. He was already on the bus. I turned to Sheriff Cross. "Thanks for bringing him back."

"You gave me a murderer and a drug dealer, so I thought it was a good trade."

"Am I going to have to come back and testify at the trial?"

"I doubt it. There's enough in those suitcases to implicate the both of them without you. Besides, I've got your contact information. I'll call you if I need you."

Sheriff Cross extended his hand, and I took it. He let go, and I watched him drive away for the last time.

Later that afternoon, with Bozeman freshly showered, he and Tommy were enjoying the sunshine on the lawn chairs. I sat on the bus steps and listened to them trade stories of the people they used to know.

Bozeman got quiet, took a swig of his beer. "Hey, Tommy, Codi told me about your condition. I'm really sorry, man. It really sucks."

Tommy slapped Bozeman's knee. "It's okay, really. I mentally prepared myself for the inevitable outcome of it a few months ago. All I want now is to get home to Los Angeles. I'd like to spend my remaining time down at Santa Monica Beach. Watch the water and the seabirds. Catch as many sunsets over the ocean as I can."

"That sounds like a lovely way to spend your time," I said. And I meant it. I was always a sucker for the ocean myself.

"Hey, Codi, when's our next gig?"

I checked the calendar on my phone. "Ten days."

"Is Los Angeles on the way?"

"It's up near Monterey, so it could be. Why?"

"I was hoping we could give Tommy a ride back to the city. Maybe see some sites, like the tar pits, or Rodeo Drive?"

"We can skip those. I've always wanted to see the Santa Monica Pier."

Bozeman smiled. "Sounds great. Done deal. Hey, are you okay, Tommy?"

"Sure, I'm just exhausted. I think I might go take a nap."

"Yeah, sure. Want me to wake you for dinner?" Bozeman asked.

"What are you having?"

"I have no clue," Bozeman said.

Tommy looked at the ground, then back at Bozeman. "Okay. It sounds delicious. I'm in."

Tommy started for his chaise, but I stopped him. "Hey Tommy, you can nap on the bus if you want to."

"No but thank you. I really like being outside. When I'm… when I'm done, I want to be outside. In the sunlight or covered in moonlight. Not cooped up in some whitewashed hospital room. Outside. In the fresh air."

Tommy dropped his head and used a slow shuffle to get around the bus. He looked tired and a lot older than he did from even the day before.

"Thanks for that. He's been through a lot," Bozeman said.

"Don't mention it. I'm happy to help." I took Tommy's words to heart and turned my chair so it faced the sun. After I had the angle just right, I sat back down, closed my eyes, and felt the warmth on my face. I loved it and vowed to do it more often. Just sit, rest, and enjoy the sun. I felt the temperature drop and guessed a passing cloud blocked the heat.

"Are you sleeping?"

I opened my eyes and saw Laurel standing before me.

"No. I'm just enjoying the sun. Do you ever sit in the sun?"

"I'm a natural redhead. If I spend over three minutes out in it, I burn like a match head."

"So, what's up?" I asked.

"I just got off the phone with Gabe. I thought you'd like to know."

"Yeah, sure. How's he doing?"

"Much, much better. You were right about the rat poison. They gave him something to counteract it, so he's recovering faster than expected."

"That's excellent news," I said.

"I've got even better news. He wants to get clean. Once he gets out of the hospital, the company's going to get him into rehab."

I smiled. "Hey, that is great news. Good for him."

"He's young. I think once he gets past this hurdle, he'll be able to do anything he wants to."

"Including being a talented drummer?" I asked.

Laurel smiled. "Well, almost anything."

"Hey, Lauren."

I rolled my eyes because I knew Bozeman was messing with her. I readjusted my chair so I could face them both.

"It's Laurel," she said.

"I know. This isn't easy for me, but Codi told me everything you did to help her help me. I want to say thank you."

Bozeman held out his hand, and Laurel took it, then moved in closer and gave him a hug. "You're welcome."

Bozeman held the hug for a moment, then let her go.

"Codi told me you have a grandmother in Bakersfield you haven't seen in a while."

"Yeah, so?"

"Hey, Codi, that's kind of near Monterey, isn't it?"

"I think we'd go right by Bakersfield on the way," I

confirmed.

"Do you think we can stop off and see Laurel's grandma?" he asked.

"Sure, we can do that. You know I'm always up for a good road trip," I said.

"Okay. We'll take you to see your grandmother. There's something you need to do for us, though."

"Sure. Anything. Name it," Laurel said.

"Well, Codi's been itching to add a fiddle player to the band, and we'd like you. Interested?"

Laurel's face beamed. "Am I interested? I'd love to."

"You'll have to sleep on the couch until we can figure out a more permanent arrangement," I said.

"That's fine with me," Laurel said.

I clapped with excitement. "All right then. I'll come over and help you pack. Then we're on the road again to our next big adventure!"

ABOUT THE AUTHOR

Dan DeKoning was born and raised in Milwaukee, Wisconsin, and currently lives in Knoxville, Tennessee with his wife and their cats.

He is a storyteller and poet who loves to write in a variety of genres and themes. He is also a voracious reader who loves to read anything he can get his hands on.

When he's not writing, you can find him hunting for treasures in used bookstores, or out exploring the planet, or geocaching, or searching for adventures and stories to tell.

ALSO BY DAN DEKONING

This is Dan DeKoning's complete library at the time of publication, but Dan has new books coming out all the time. Sign up for his newsletter at DanDeKoning.com to stay up to date on new releases.

Fiction
Déjà Vu
The Haunting of Hyacinth House
How Deep the Darkness

Geocaching Mystery Series
The Cacheland Conspiracy
The Quincy Bay Quandary
The Secret of the Seven Valleys
The Geocaching Mystery Omnibus – Volume 1

Codi Cassidy Cozy Mystery Series
Acoustics and Alibis
Ballads and Bloodshed
Codas and Calibers
Codi Cassidy Cozy Omnibus – Volume 1

Poetry Collections
Lost and Found
Random Thoughts

www.ingramcontent.com/pod-product-compliance
Lightning Source LLC
Chambersburg PA
CBHW061534310726
48972CB00008B/2457